I locked the bedroom door, set the lamp on the dresser and went to the window. The panes were rattling from the force of the wind and I could make out the bleak skeletons of the dead trees as the wind whipped their naked branches. Then I felt the castle move—and the lamp began to slide off the dresser. The ancient house seemed to be alive. There were sounds everywhere and always that moaning and groaning that seemed to come from walls, floors and ceilings. There was nothing human in that terrible wailing. . . .

WITCH'S CASTLE

Dorothy Daniels

WARNER

PAPERBACK LIBRARY
NEW YORK

WARNER PAPERBACK LIBRARY EDITION

First Printing: November, 1971
Second Printing: August, 1972

*Warner Paperback Library is a division of Warner Books, Inc.,
315 Park Avenue South, New York, N.Y. 10010*

ONE

The car was ancient and wheezy. It was without a top, which was just as well, for I had it heaped high with all the apparatus I required for my work. However, I was half frozen, for this was September in the northern reaches of the Atlantic off the Maine coast.

The road was winding, to avoid the marshy land left by the tide. At changing hours of the day and night, the road was under tidewater, so that it was half washed-out all the time.

Behind me lay the village in which everyone on this island lived. It was a very old and weather-beaten village, but its buildings were so solidly constructed that they still withstood the ravages of time. It was strictly a summer resort and the season, which began on Memorial Day weekend, ended promptly on Labor Day, after which the village folded its wings and slept until the following season. Now the place had a lonely and desolate air, which I welcomed. I was eager to begin my work, and once started, I'd not welcome interruptions.

The mainland, nearly hidden now by a fog that was beginning to creep in from the sea, was busy and industrial. These industries were one reason why I was here at this uncomfortable time of year. The other reason was that the channel between the island and the mainland was full of plankton, protozoa, bacteria, aquatic plant life, clams, oysters, lobsters, many kinds of fish and . . . poison.

I was here, you see, to do some research for my doctoral thesis in marine biology. At the age of twenty-two, I was pretty much the baby of that year's crop of Ph.D. candidates—Gale Dexter, Girl Wonder, as my father called me teasingly. I didn't mind. I'd worked hard in college and at the university, and I wasn't about to slack off now.

Something rattled ominously in the back of the car. I prayed that it wasn't any of my precious glassware, because it wouldn't be easy to replace a broken article of my portable laboratory. Not up here, and especially not through any cooperation I could get from the villagers, which was practically nil.

The tract of land bore the not-very-reassuring name of Witch's Island because of some ancient history, with which I was not familiar, regarding the presence of witches. Especially one particular witch. I was heading for the castle, so-called, in which she'd lived and—I hoped—died, some generations ago (about 1870, I'd been told. So she was a late-generation witch). Some say she still lived in the old house she'd had built for herself and her coven of witches.

The island was shaped like a huge comma: rounded at one end, then narrowing as it stretched to a point so far from the village that the end of it couldn't be seen because of the slopes and gullies. I was heading for the point.

Nobody lived there—except the witch or her ghostly remains—I'd been informed with a derisive glance. Which gives some idea of how well I was regarded in the island village, and on the mainland as well, for that matter. Everything habitable in the village was either occupied by its permanent residents or was open only during the summer months, so that a stranger had nowhere to go except to the mainland, and my work wouldn't permit that.

The car plowed through a shallow pond of tidewater, sending gulls squawking in protest. After I got the car righted and aimed along the somewhat indistinct road, I saw the castle.

I braked, slowed and then stopped because I couldn't believe it. I'd seen this place from the ocean a few times, but never up close. At a distance, it had seemed to possess a certain charm, reminiscent of the Gothic era. Now it appeared more like an apparition of a house, for it was surrounded by dead, wind-washed trees. A huge, square, quietly decaying monstrosity, it was done in jigsaw Gothic with bay windows and a glassed-in turret. It had a front porch and two side porches. I expect there was a back one too. I also knew the property sloped down to a good-sized pier.

I'd been informed that the house was in excellent condition, that there was running water, and that it was furnished. It had been repaired and partly refurnished by the former owner who'd lived there only a total of nine weeks, then left precipitously, to the amusement of the island villagers. I leased it from a grinning Mr. Abrams, who rented houses for the owners and whose office was in the fishing-tackle store he operated. He had set an absurdly low rent, stating since it was out of season and since I was a student, he'd not take advantage. Only later did I learn he'd set up a pool, with the jackpot going to the one who guessed closest to the hour I'd come flying back to the village.

I'd been told it was a journey of three miles from this tip of the island back to the village and that I'd be the lone dweller in this great privacy except for a man who had leased the only summer cottage on the point, about a quarter of a mile to the south of the castle. Nobody knew much about him, but he seemed to have money and spent it freely, which was recommendation enough for the natives. And—he stayed to himself.

That was good news. What I sought more than anything else, at this particular time, was solitude so I might complete the research on my thesis and, incidentally, add a little something to improve the ecology of the region.

I stopped the car in the barren, open area before the front porch and regarded the place speculatively. I wondered if I'd been wise in renting a place so isolated, and for a few moments, I was tempted to abandon my thesis. But then, reason prevailed. I'd worked too many years for the final degree I wanted. Isolation, I reminded myself, lent for complete concentration.

I got out of the car and walked slowly to the porch. To my surprise, the steps were sturdy. I had a key, but I didn't need it. The front door wasn't locked. I stepped into a deep, wide reception hall complete with a chandelier and candle-tipped electric bulbs. My spirits lifted at the sight of them, for once I'd glimpsed the place, I expected I'd have to move about after dark with either candles or lamps. I reached out and flicked the switch. Nothing happened. Then I realized I should have spoken to Mr. Abrams about having the electricity turned on. It meant a trip to town tomorrow, but it was only a minor interruption.

I moved deeper into the reception hall. Despite the warmth of my wool sweater and slacks, I felt chilled, and I knew why. The house and its interior reminded me of

8

one of those old-time movie horror stories they show on television about two in the morning. If an assortment of bats had come swooping down on me, I wouldn't have been surprised.

But the mood quickly left me as I started an inspection, for the place was remarkably clean. There was not even a trace of dust, although the last family living here had left a year ago. I faced a wide, sweeping staircase that led to a balconied second floor. From where I stood, it was so dark, I believed it must be windowless. I made a hasty inspection tour of the first floor. There was a living room and, adjoining it, a smaller and rather cozy room, which was evidently used as a family room. There was also a fair-sized library, with walls shelved from ceiling to floor and fairly well filled. On the opposite side was the dining room, joined to the kitchen by a large pantry. All the rooms were high-ceilinged and spacious. The furnishings were mostly heavy maple, with chintz-covered cushions. Certainly, the outside had given no hint of the charm of the interior. Pleasantly relieved, I decided to investigate the second floor.

The stairs and hall were uncarpeted, and my footsteps echoed hollowly through the house, creating an eerie feeling. A creaking sound, slow but measured, made me pause. I wondered if someone might have taken possession of the place, unaware it had been rented. I called out a greeting, but there was no answer. I called out again, asking if someone was about. The squeaking stopped, but no voice answered.

I cautioned myself not to let my imagination play games with me, and I proceeded with my observation of the house. The hall was long and wide, with eight doors, all of them closed. I paused midway along it and regarded the window at the far end. A shaft of sunlight helped to light the gloomy interior; yet I felt the place had a melancholy air, enhanced by the walls paneled from

9

floor to ceiling in dark wood, lavishly and intricately carved.

Of the eight doors leading into the rooms, five were on one side, three on the other. Seven were bedrooms of varying size. I chose the largest, for it was adequately furnished in mahogany, which gleamed from many polishings. The four-poster was covered with a snow-white candlewick bedspread, attesting to the cleanliness of the bed linens beneath it. The windows sparkled, and the tie-back curtains, nicely starched, gave off a newly washed fragrance.

It was almost as if the room had been prepared for my coming, yet I'd not been informed that anyone had been hired to take care of the housework. Nonetheless, I was pleased. There was one more room on the floor for me to inspect, the one adjoining my bedroom. I returned to the hall and went to the final door. I opened it, stepped inside and stopped short. I don't know what I noticed first, so great was my surprise. But it was a sewing room, with several dressmaker dummies set in a row. They differed in size, from one quite heavy female form to that of a child of, perhaps, eleven. The floor was bare, but the walls were decorated with framed drawings of costumes from the latter part of the nineteenth century. My glance shifted back to the dressmaker dummies. The clothes were similar to the drawings. I moved closer to them. They were very old, but instead of a musty smell, there was the clinging scent of lavender, as if someone gave them loving care. Yet the material was faded, and though my hand reached out to touch one quite-elegant gown, I hesitated, lest it disintegrate at my touch.

The skirts were trained and heavily embroidered. Some were encrusted with varicolored stones. On closer inspection, I noticed the silks had cracked with age. The miracle was that they had survived. Regarding these period costumes, I felt as if I had been transported back in the pages of history, and I got the sudden idea I was not alone. As if to assure me of it, the creaking sound began again. I knew now it was a floor board. I turned slowly, not certain what to expect.

A gasp of surprise escaped me as my eyes regarded the far end of the room where there was a dais. On it was a figure seated in a rocker. I was certain it was a dummy, for it was motionless, except for the sway of the chair. The figure was small and delicate. The face, at this distance, seemed carved of porcelain, yet there was a sparkle to the blue eyes and I thought I saw the lids close and open. I walked slowly the length of the room. I noted the slender hands, with heavily ringed fingers, which rested on the arms of the chair. The rocking didn't cease, nor did the eyes shift their gaze as I approached. Mine didn't either, for that matter, for I was fascinated. Perhaps even hypnotized. A wig, with curls which touched the shoulders, set atop the small head.

I reached the dais and paused. Once again I took in the heavily skirted costume of magenta. I still didn't know if I was gazing at a live member of my own sex or a cleverly made dummy. And yet, with the measured rocking, the figure had to be a human. I glanced at the hands, noted the prominent blue veins and was more certain of it.

"Hello," I said. "I'm Gale Dexter. Who are you?"

Her lips pursed in disappointment. "Didn't I frighten you?"

I smiled. "Startled would be a better word. You look much too lovely to frighten anyone."

"I'd hoped to frighten you away from here," she said, with a little sigh. But I admire courage, so I'm glad you're staying. Does your room please you?"

"Then you know I've already inspected it."

She arose and lifted her skirts, revealing magenta satin slippers decorated with rosettes. She made her way to

11

the single step at one side of the dais. "Oh yes," she replied. "I heard you moving about."

"Why didn't you answer me when I called out?"

"As I said, I'd hoped to frighten you away from here."

"Why should you wish to do that?"

"Because I enjoy the castle and I don't want it lived in by others."

"Do you live here?"

"Sometimes. That is, when no one else is here and no one else ever is—for very long."

Her smile was complacent, and though I extended a hand to assist her down the step, she disdained it. I marveled that she could manage with the voluminous skirt. She moved gracefully, and when she stood before me, I felt much taller than my five feet seven, for then she did have to look up at me.

"You still haven't told me your name," I said.

"Do you really want to know?"

"Very much," I assured her.

She looked pleased. "Mary Selwich. Some of the old-timers call me Crazy Mary. The young people are more tolerant."

I was startled by her statement. "Why should anyone be so unkind as to call you that?"

"Perhaps, after you're here a while, you'll call me that too."

"Believe me, I shan't."

"Because you respect the aged?"

"You don't look old," I said sincerely. "There isn't a line in your face."

"I'm nigh onto seventy-five," she replied serenely. "Perhaps older. When one reaches that age, a few years one way or the other doesn't make much difference, do they?"

"I think you can be proud of it," I replied.

She looked pleased. "I keep this castle up, you know."

"All by yourself?"

"Oh yes. I don't believe the owners know about it. As for Mr. Abrams, he doesn't mind."

"Doesn't he recompense you for your work?"

Her hands raised in protest. "I wouldn't take money."

I regarded the frail figure. "I don't think you should be doing housework."

"Oh yes, I should," she said. "It keeps me limber and I feel it gives me the right to come here when I wish. I like it here. It's like a second home."

"I'm glad you feel that way," I replied. "And so long as I'm here, I'd like you to stay."

Her forefinger touched her brow in a thoughtful attitude. "I shall think about it. Of course, I do have a little house on the edge of the village and most of the time I live there."

"Just remember you're welcome. You'll have to excuse me now. I have a car to unpack."

"You may go, my dear."

I thanked her, managing to repress a smile. I felt as if I'd been dismissed by royalty. I could see she played a game here and I wondered where she'd found the clothes. In the attic, I supposed. I saw no harm in her indulging herself. Apparently the attic was filled with trunks of garments worn by former owners and Mary Selwich had discovered them. Certainly she was doing no harm, and if she derived a little pleasure in dressing up and pretending she was someone else, no one was hurt. By keeping the castle clean, she earned the right to play with its treasures. I promptly forgot about Mary Selwich and went downstairs and out to the car, now thoroughly pleased by my surroundings and eager to begin work.

13

TWO

I began lugging my gear inside. It was no easy task. The laboratory, in several sections, was heavy with apparatus and bottles filled with chemicals. Then there were the hydrographic collecting bottles, a junior-sized autoclave which I wondered how I'd operate, for it was heated by electricity. My microscopes were in neat cases and presented no problem. The plankton nets were bulky, but light, though the pumps were backbreakers.

I was a true scientist all right, for I brought in my personal luggage last, though it consisted only of an overnight bag. I closed the door because the air was crisp even at this hour just preceding noon. I opened blinds, gingerly drew back drapes that looked as if they'd fall apart if moved, though they survived very well. Next, I selected a room to be used as my laboratory. Because I required running water, I chose the kitchen.

It had counters, many shelves and a spacious pantry with even more shelves. It would serve well. If I had to do my cooking in between the microscopes and the collecting apparatus, that would be fine with me.

I began setting up. I had unpacked most of the reagent bottles, relieved to find them all intact, and I lined these on the pantry shelves in neat rows. I was digging out some of the apparatus when I heard what sounded like a muffled explosion. I listened again, but it was not repeated so I went back to work, wondering briefly if Mary Selwich was still trying to frighten me away.

About three minutes later, there was a roar. I rushed to the front door, threw it open and stared in awe at my wheezy 1958 Dodge, now one big ball of fire. The tires were flaming and smoking, the gas tank had exploded, and in minutes there'd be just a hot skeleton of a car remaining.

I felt completely frustrated. Not because I loved that car, but I needed it. Now I'd have to rely on my motorboat, still tied up in the village. Trouble was, the boat was there and I was here, and I didn't look forward to a three-mile hike over these tidelands with much pleasure.

There was nothing I could do except watch it burn, so I thought I might as well enjoy the destruction of two hundred and ninety dollars' worth of automobile. I thanked my stars I'd succeeded in getting everything out of it before the fire started.

That gave me a jolt. How had the fire started? How does a fire begin in a car that has been standing idle for at least half an hour? Even with a gas leak, there'd be no sparks, no hot wires. The idea that it might have been deliberately set gave me a few moments of apprehension. I dismissed the thought, though with some effort. I was completely aware the villagers didn't like what I was doing, but certainly none of them would resort to this. What would they gain, anyway? Unless my boat was burned too. That would really put me out of business.

16

Mary Selwich came to mind, and I wondered if she could have done this. Was she the gentle lady that she seemed? I recalled her nickname, yet I couldn't believe she'd even know how to set a car afire. Nonetheless, I went inside and called her name. There was no answer, so I went upstairs.

The sewing room was empty. The dummies were nude and there was no trace of their costumes. I called her name again and again as I walked along the corridor to go downstairs, but there was no answer. I was about to inspect each of the rooms when I heard a roar of sound from outside.

I went downstairs and opened the front door. The sound grew louder and I knew it was a souped-up motor. I stepped onto the porch just as the motorcycle and its rider appeared from what was left of the road that led to the shore. It must be the man who'd been living in the cottage there alone for some time. Evidently I was going to meet him whether I wished to or not.

The wheels of his bike tore up clam shells, sand, little stones and some turf as it came barreling toward me. He braked, hopped off, set the stand and walked in my direction.

I was quite surprised, because I'd imagined some red-faced, elderly fisherman. Instead the man who approached was no more than twenty-five years old, tall and slim, with good shoulders. His hair was a reddish-brown and cut fairly short, though he sported long sideburns. Even from a distance, I could see the clear blueness of his eyes. To my mind, he was quite handsome, with a generous mouth and facial crinkles to indicate he smiled a lot.

"I guess I'm too late," he said, looking at the smouldering remains of the car.

"Not even a fully equipped fire department could have done anything with that mess," I said.

He stood quietly, regarding the last of the fire. There

being nothing for me to do, I sat on the porch steps and we both stared at the destruction.

He glanced at me. "My name is Randall. Roger."

"I'm Gale Dexter."

"I know. Heard all about you in the village. You're the bug hunter who's going to give the island a bad name."

"Bug hunter," I said scornfully. "That's a really good idea of what they know about my work. I'm a marine biologist. I'm working on my thesis and my subject is to be the effects of industrial and domestic waste on the channel waters around this island. My home base is Woods Hole, where I hope I'm going to teach some day."

"A marine biologist," he mused. "That's an odd profession for such an attractive girl."

"I like to think it's an important one." I couldn't keep irritation from edging my voice. "We'd better do something about the ecology of this nation soon or we'll all go down in one big wave of pollution."

His smile was apologetic. "I didn't mean to irritate you. You're right, of course."

I stood up, far from being appeased. "Are you merely being polite, or are you truly concerned by what's already happened?"

"Being from New York City, I'm truly concerned, Miss Dexter. No one lives there long without being aware of the pollution in the atmosphere."

"There's also the pollution being poured into lakes and oceans, contaminating sea life."

He nodded. "I know that's what you're working on."

"Just how do you know, Mr. Randall?"

"I've really riled you, haven't I?"

"Yes. I take my work very seriously. It merits that."

"I'm not arguing the merits of your work. I admire you, both your persistence and your spirit. As to how I know about you—it's no secret in the village as to what you're doing here."

18

"I didn't intend it should be."

"You didn't intend to rile the natives either."

"Are you implying they'd resort to violence to frighten me into leaving?"

He shrugged. "No telling. They're dead against your staying here. They believe you're going to give the fishing and lobstering industries a black mark. Since the village exists on products that come from the sea, they have reason to be afraid."

"I agree. Especially with that chemical manufacturing plant up the mainland coast and the oil-cracking plant just above that."

"What do you expect to find?"

"Mercury in the livers of fish taken from the channel. DDT in the plankton, the protozoa, in oyster beds. The usual. But I've not really begun."

He whistled softly. "Bad as that?"

I nodded. "When I've completed my tests, I intend to make a formal declaration of my findings."

"That's what the villagers are afraid of. That's why they want you off this island. Or did you know?"

I managed a smile. "I know they resent my presence."

He returned the smile. "Well, I don't. And I like your smile. Especially that one dimple in your cheek. It belies the fact that you're a scientist."

I sobered. "What do you mean?"

"It gives you a flirty look."

"Believe me, Mr. Randall, I am not the flirty type."

He spoke with mock seriousness. "I've already discovered that, Miss Dexter. But just in case you should meet with another accident—heaven forbid—would you mind telling me where you hail from?"

"It wasn't *I* who met with an accident," I said.

"So it wasn't." He regarded the car and moved over to observe the marker plate. "Pennsylvania. Mining section or farming section?"

19

"What difference does it make?" I countered, a little unnerved by the directness of his approach.

"Merely a matter of interest." He returned to my side. "I'd say farming."

I couldn't help but smile. "A little place just outside of York."

He looked reflective. "Rolling, verdant hills, cows grazing in the pasture, spanking white house, spanking red barn—just like a Grandma Moses painting."

"Sort of," I said, my voice softening at the memory. "Sheep graze there too. It's all very bucolic."

"Brothers or sisters?"

"No."

"I haven't either. But both my parents are living."

"So are mine." I laughed. "You have a way of getting information out of people, haven't you?"

"I have a naturally curious mind," he replied.

"So have I," I said. "I'd like to know what you're doing here. I might add, so would the villagers."

It was his turn to laugh. "Oh, I'm just biding my time. It's pleasant here—particularly now, with the summer tourists gone."

"I know. You're a recently returned veteran and you've come here to find yourself. How am I guessing?"

"Lousy. Oh, I did the Vietnam bit—about the time of the Spanish-American War, as I look back now. No, I have a job. I'm on leave—sort of—just felt I wanted to get away."

I gave him an appraising glance. "You're trying to recover from a broken romance."

He burst into laughter and I knew I'd guessed wrong again. He said, "I've yet to meet the girl."

"Maybe you're too particular."

"Maybe," he agreed. "Or maybe I've just been too busy. Is that your reason?"

"What makes you think I haven't met someone special?"

"Your no-nonsense look," he said. "You have an interesting face, good bone structure. Chin a bit stubborn perhaps, gray eyes a little cold, but that dimple softens the overall effect."

"Never mind, Mr. Randall, you've made your point."

"Have I, really?" His eyes regarded me speculatively. "You're making me out to be a cold fish."

"Are you?" he asked with a half smile.

"Yes."

"I don't believe it," he retorted. "Not with that auburn hair. I suppose you keep it cut short because you haven't time to fuss with it."

"Right. Now please excuse me, I've got to finish unpacking."

"I've angered you again."

"You haven't," I said. "I just have no more time to bandy words."

"You're right, of course. And I'll admit I was doing everything to keep you out here. But don't be too tough on me. I'm a little afraid of a marine biologist. I just don't want you catching me in a net and placing me under your microscope to determine what kind of character I really am by what my macronucleus is, my food vacuoles, my chromosomes. . . ."

I forgot my anger in my surprise. "So you do know something about biology."

"Little enough. Did you bring your underwater gear?"

"It's in the boat, which is back at the marina."

"Good. We'll have to go diving together one day." He was eying the now-cooling wreckage of the car. "Excuse me a moment."

He went down to the car and poked around the skeleton for a few moments. He came back with part of a bottle in his hand.

"This was wired to the underpart of the car," he said. "I've seen them before. The North Vietnamese used to attach them to cars. They were crude compared to this, but they went off the same."

"What in the world are you talking about?" I asked.

"This, my lady marine biologist, is a form of fire bomb. It's attached to some part of the car. The fuse is a combination of chemicals that react slowly upon one another. The timing can be exactly measured if need be. When it goes off, there's a flash; the fuel contained in the bottle explodes into flame and whatever it is attached to explodes into ruins, as you can readily see."

I felt all of that self-confidence with which I'd bolstered my courage slip away from me.

"Mr. Randall, you must be mistaken."

"Do you drive around with a Pepsi bottle hooked to the undercarriage of your car?"

"No. But who would want to kill me?"

"Apparently they don't want to kill you. If you were in the car, you could have jumped out before the flames spread to the gas tank. If they'd wanted to kill you, the bottle would have been filled with explosive, and you wouldn't have had a chance. Maybe," he went on, "if this warning doesn't work, they will use explosive."

"I'm—I just don't get it."

"It's not a scientific explanation, Miss Dexter, but it's not an involved one either. You're here to study life in the ocean. If it's affected somehow by outpourings of chemicals and waste, you're going to make that public. The fishing and lobstering industries are suffering now because of the revelations of ecologists. The village people don't want that to happen here, so they're taking steps to see it does not. In other words, this is an invitation for you to go home."

"I'll not give up my work," I said. "I will not be frightened away. I leased this house and I'll stay here until my work is done."

"Miss Dexter," he said as he arose, "this is serious

22

business to the villagers—and to the industries you're going to condemn. These people play for keeps. See you later."

He walked away, flinging the broken bottle into the burned-out car. I watched him climb aboard his motorcycle and go off in a cloud of dust. I entered the house and closed the door.

Suddenly I felt as if I'd just sprung a trap and locked myself in.

THREE

By late afternoon, I had everything arranged to my satisfaction so I could start work in the morning. Then I recalled that I had little food with me and I would have to go back to the village for more. I also had to bring my boat here before someone attached a fire bomb to it. The hulk of the burned car was a reminder I could be in considerable danger.

With the setting-up finished, my thoughts turned to Mr. Randall. I was sorry that I'd been abrupt and, perhaps, rude to him, but then, I had no time for men. Not even a young and personable one with a mysterious air and a very inquisitive nature.

Upstairs, I again inspected my bedroom with adjoining bath. I'd be quite comfortable here except that I'd have to be content with lamplight. Back in the corridor, my attention was drawn to the closed door of the sewing room. The expanse of wall in the hall seemed longer than the room. Curious, I opened the door and observed the far end of the room. It certainly didn't extend the length of the hall, yet there was no door leading to another room beyond it.

I banged my fist on the blank wall, but all I did was make my hand tingle from the impact. It didn't seem that there was space behind that wall, for there was no hollow sound. It didn't interest me enough to pursue the problem, so I went downstairs again.

Though there was no electricity, at least I had a range with compressed gas. I opened a large can of soup, a package of crackers, and made instant coffee. While I ate, I studied the textbooks from which I drew my methods and techniques. I found some old oil lamps in the pantry, on a high shelf. They were dusty and dirty, but the reservoirs contained kerosene. I cleaned them, trimmed the blackened wicks as expertly as if I'd lived a hundred years ago. When I lit them, I had a fairly well illuminated workbench, though I didn't know what I'd do for the powerful light needed by my microscopes, especially the phase one, until the electricity was turned on.

I studied until my eyelids drooped. I didn't quite realize the reason for my intense diligence until I was ascending the staircase, carrying one of the oil lamps. Then I knew. The vastness and stillness of Witch's Castle was more than a little unnerving. Yet I wasn't afraid. I'd grown up in a rambling farmhouse with thoroughly modern parents. Dad was a gentleman farmer, and both he and mother were active in social and charity activities. While I'd been raised with love, I'd not been coddled. Life on a farm is an education in itself, and I'd been encouraged to think and do for myself at an early age.

But I'd never felt so alone before. I suppose it was a combination of the isolation of the house and its emptiness which seemed to close in around me. That, coupled with

26

what had happened to my car this afternoon, lowered my spirits. I switched my thoughts to the cheery farmhouse and visualized my mother and dad seated contentedly before the glowing fireplace—perhaps even now discussing the project I was involved in and feeling a modest parental pride in my efforts.

In my room, I creamed my face, washed it and got into a fleece grannie nightie. The warmth of it felt good against the already chilled night air, for the room was actually cold.

I blew out the lamp and walked over to the window to raise it a few inches. I liked fresh air while I slept, even if it was chilled. As my eyes adjusted to the darkness, I was able to view the bleakness of the island tip; the barren trees now bore a sinister look. I got into bed, shivering between the icy sheets, but the woolen blanket and comforter of down held in my body heat and I gradually relaxed.

I felt more secure now and believed the slight attack of nerves had been brought on by fatigue. I lay there and made plans for the following day. I'd arise at my usual early hour and hike back to the village. No doubt Mr. Randall would ride me there, but I didn't wish to ask a favor of him. Besides, I wasn't sure I could hang onto the back of his motorbike on the narrow, rutted road.

So I'd walk—hopeful the tide would be out because I didn't want to wade either. I'd purchase supplies and stow them on the boat. The remainder of my luggage was at the hotel. The thought of the trip back by boat pleased me. Both the boat and the engine were in fine condition. This, of course, would occupy much of my day. However, with luck, there might be time to set a few underwater plates to which barnacles and sea worms would adhere for later collection and examination. I wanted to get started as quickly as possible. And with that thought in mind, I drifted off to sleep.

I was awakened by a horrible wail, half shriek and half moan. For a few moments I lay there, confused and disoriented. Then I remembered where I was and as I did, that terrible sound filled the house again. And then words were being spoken.

A voice, hollow and demanding, said, "Come to me, Belial. I am your daughter. I say, come to me! Come to me!"

The words were spoken over and over and they resounded through the house. I sat up, thoroughly awake now, prickles of fear covering my skin. I couldn't lie here and listen to it. I didn't know if the voice was male or female, but I knew its purpose was to frighten me into abandoning Witch's Castle. Slow anger replaced my fear as my hand explored the bedside table for the box of matches I'd set there. I found them, struck one and lit the lamp.

I got out of bed, dressed quickly, pushing my feet into square-toed walking shoes. I tossed a cape over my shoulders, picked up the lamp and stepped into the corridor. But the moment I opened my door, the voice stopped and not a sound disturbed the quiet of the house.

I again thought of Mary Selwich and wished I'd inquired about her in the village. It had to be she, and she was once again playing her little game, attempting to frighten me away from here. She considered the castle her own private domain. She'd probably even frightened away the present owners who were, no doubt, now trying to unload their white elephant.

I'd not be frightened by Mary. I called out, "Miss Selwich, if you're in one of the bedrooms, come out. I want no more of this nonsense."

There was no answer and I repeated what I'd said before. Again, I was greeted by silence. I began a check of each bedroom and the adjoining closets. They were all devoid of clothing, so it took only a moment to hold my lamp in their dark interior. I even got on my knees and looked under each bed to see if little Miss Selwich was playing a game of hide and seek.

I was irritated with myself that I'd left the sewing room for last because that was undoubtedly where she was awaiting me. Probably once again seated on the dais, dressed in a period costume of the last century.

I opened the door, calling her name as I did so. I stepped into the room, holding my lamp high as I moved deeper into it. The dummies were unclad, the dais held only the empty rocking chair. Except for two ancient sewing machines and a few scattered straight-backed chairs, the room was devoid of furnishings, making it an impossible place for concealment.

I thought of the attic and wondered how one gained access to it. Then I remembered seeing a narrow door in the butler's pantry. Perhaps beyond it was a stairway which led directly up to the attic. I hoped so. I was eager to find Mary Selwich. It had to be she, and she had to be told I'd not countenance this foolishness.

I was halfway down the stairs when the stillness of the house was again broken by a horrible, blood-chilling shriek —not of pain, but of an ugly strange triumph. I gripped the rail and stood there, too terrified to move. I looked about me, but all I could see were grotesque shadows caused by my lamp. The unholy shriek continued without let-up and I knew I wanted only one thing—escape from this house. It had been aptly named Witch's Castle. The place seemed filled with the hellishness of one accursed.

I gathered my courage and moved down the steps as fast as I could, not stopping until my fumbling fingers had unlocked the door. Still holding the lamp and running now, I crossed the porch, went down the steps and headed for the area where I knew Mr. Randall's cabin was.

The burned-out ruins of the car seemed to mock me as

I passed it. My heart pounded madly as I ran, but from fear, not exertion. I couldn't believe such a thing could happen or that I would be so terrified by it. Yet I had just one thought in mind—to get to Mr. Randall. He was the only one I could go to, not just because he was close by, but, even in my terror, I knew I'd receive short shrift from the villagers. They might even have put Mary Selwich up to it. I was ashamed to think the antics of a frail little seventy-five-year-old lady could have sent me flying out of the house.

I was breathless when I finally reached the cabin, but relieved when I saw light streaming through a window. I called out Mr. Randall's name. His door opened immediately, sending more welcoming light my way. He stepped outside, and when he saw my lamp, he strode briskly in my direction. He reached me none too soon, for I was about ready to collapse. I tried to talk, but in my haste, the words were a jumble of sound.

"Easy now," he said. He took the lamp from me, put an arm about my waist and guided me to the cabin. Once inside, he placed the lamp on the table, eased me into a deep leather chair and went over to a cabinet. He took out a bottle of brandy, poured a little in a glass and brought it to me. I shook my head, for I needed more than brandy to reassure me.

"Drink it," he commanded. "Sip it anway. It will steady you."

I took the glass, feeling that if I didn't, he'd tilt my head and pour the liquid down my throat.

"Don't talk right away," he said. "Settle back in the chair. You're trembling."

He closed the door, then sat beside me on the large leather footrest. He took my hand which rested on the arm of the chair and held it between both of his. I started to put the glass on the table alongside me.

"Finish it," he said.

30

Once again I obeyed, for I realized his firmness, plus the brandy, was exactly what I needed.

"Now put the glass down and tell me what happened," he said.

I sighed and rested my head against the leather back of the chair. "I was awakened by a horrible scream—or a cry—or a shriek . . . I don't exactly know how to describe it, but it seemed to have come straight from hell."

"Did someone enter the castle?" he asked.

"Someone must have," I replied. "A voice—I couldn't recognize whether it was a man's or a woman's—called on Belial to come. It said, 'I am your daughter. Come to me. Come to me.'"

"Are you sure you didn't have a nightmare?" he asked in a voice tinged with incredulity.

"Positive," I retorted. "I got up, dressed and checked the second floor. I thought Mary Selwich was playing another game." His smile of disbelief irritated me. "It's true, I tell you." I tried to pull my hand free of his, but he kept a firm grip on it.

"I'm not laughing at you," he said. "I know you're very upset. But Miss Mary couldn't frighten a humming-bird."

"Oh yes, she could," I retorted. "She gave me quite a start today when I entered the castle. She said she wanted to frighten me from the castle. She didn't want anyone living there."

"Do you know anything about her other than what you've heard in the village?"

"I never heard a word about her in the village. I didn't know of her existence until I found her in the sewing room of the castle."

He nodded. "I'm afraid she considers you an inter-loper."

31

"Don't you think it's the other way around?" I demanded.

He arose, stirred the embers of the dying fire in the fireplace and placed another log on the andirons. It caught almost at once, the outer bark crackling as it flamed.

He turned back to me. "I can't imagine anyone resenting Miss Mary."

"I don't resent her," I said patiently. "I resent her trying to frighten me."

"I can't believe she'd do such a thing," he said.

I stood up. "I won't take up any more of your time, Mr. Randall. And thanks for being so kind."

"You can't go yet. Just before you came, I put a pot of coffee on. It must be about ready to perc."

He went out to the kitchen and returned to report it would be ready in five minutes. He motioned me back to the chair and he resumed his seat on the footstool.

"You must have propane gas too," I said.

"Mostly everyone does on the island," he replied.

"I noticed the woodbin is filled. Whom do I thank for that?"

"Me," he replied. "I filled it for you. You'll also find the fireplaces set up in the library and living room."

"My thanks," I said.

"Weren't you surprised to find the castle so immaculate?"

"You can't take credit for that. Miss Selwich told me she kept it up."

"She gives it tender, loving care. I believe it's a sort of sanctuary for her."

"Why should she need one?"

"I don't really know. Loneliness, perhaps. Also, she won't believe the story regarding the woman who lived there a hundred years ago and who was professed to be a witch."

"Certainly, she isn't afraid there. Did she know you cut the firewood?"

"Oh yes," he replied with that easy smile. "We're rather good friends."

"Does she have any friends in the village?"

He sobered. "No. They regard her as an eccentric."

"She told me what they called her."

His mouth tightened with annoyance. "It's damn rotten of them. She minds her own business and keeps up the castle. Without her, Mr. Abrams would have to pay someone to come out here and do it."

"Who owns the place?"

"A California family. But they didn't stay out the season. They claimed the witch drove them out of there."

"How ridiculous," I scoffed. "It has to be Miss Selwich."

"Have you heard the legend regarding the castle?"

"No, and I'm not interested."

"Since you intend to continue living there—or do you?"

"I do," I said firmly.

"Then you should know it." He stood up. "While we drink our coffee, I'll tell you."

I arose. "Let me help you."

"Come along."

I followed him to the kitchen. It was small, neat and sparsely but adequately furnished. He removed the pot from the flame and set it aside for the grounds to settle. I got two mugs from one of the shelves.

"Cream or black?" he asked.

"Black," I said.

He filled our cups and we returned to the living room. The log was burning brightly, sending out welcoming warmth. We resumed our seats and Mr. Randall started his story.

"The castle was once owned and lived in by a woman who was professed to be a witch. There are many ugly

33

stories about her still prevalent in the village and on the mainland."

"Such as," I prompted.

"She was reputed to have caused children to sicken and herds of milk cows to die; to create accidents which befell people she'd placed a curse on. Finally, the villagers decided they'd had enough. They went to the castle en masse, bringing a rope with which to lynch her. However, they found only an empty house. There wasn't a trace of the woman. She had literally vanished. They said she'd disappeared from the face of the earth through her powers of witchcraft which made them fear her more than ever, for they believed one day she'd be back. Witches are never supposed to die, you know."

I couldn't help but smile. "You're telling it to me as if you believe it."

"That the woman was a witch or that they tried to lynch her?" he asked.

"Oh, I'm familiar with mob rule, so I believe the lynching part, but not that she was a witch. Tell me, was it her powers of witchcraft that caused her to know they were coming to lynch her?"

"I'm not trying to inject myself into the story so far as the villagers or their ancestors are concerned."

"But I'm curious about this story—and yes, interested."

"Interested in tearing it to pieces," he said flatly.

"Exactly." I took a sip of the steaming liquid and decided to let it cool a bit more. "If she was possessed of such horrifying gifts, why didn't she wipe out the villagers with one sweep of her broom?"

He didn't laugh at my attempt at facetiousness. "It was claimed she'd had a falling out with the devil."

I shrugged impatiently. "Oh, wow."

"Nevertheless, I'll finish the story," he said. "When the frustrated mob couldn't find her, they tried to burn down the house. Only the house wouldn't burn. By daylight you can see for yourself the seared wood beneath the north porch, which is where they lit the fire. When it refused to stay lit, it became part of the legend."

I sipped my coffee thoughtfully. "Why are you telling me all this?"

"To get you out of that house."

"Why should you want to?"

This time his smile was almost reluctant. "I suppose I'm concerned about your safety there."

"Because of the witch?"

"Because of what happened to your car."

"Do you believe the villagers are responsible?" I asked.

"I don't know. Did you notify the constable?"

"No," I said.

"Why not?"

"I know I'm unpopular here. I want to remain until my work is completed."

"You could stay at the hotel," he suggested.

"I'd be no more popular there," I said. "Besides, it's closed until next season."

He nodded. "I forgot. But the castle's so isolated."

"It's what I wanted."

"Plus a galloping case of terror," he said dryly.

"I'm over it," I said. "And I still think it was the work of Mary Selwich. If she didn't do it herself, she probably got some mischievous teenager to do it for her. When I go back, I'm going to check the attic. It's quite possible there's an opening up there which could lead down to the fireplace in my bedroom. A voice, calling down, could have had an echoing effect."

We both arose. I brought the cups out to the kitchen, rinsed them and placed them on the drainboard.

"Before you go, there's one more thing you should know."

"About the witch?" I asked, smiling.

He didn't return the smile. "Her name was Sarah Dexter."

I sobered. "So that's it. It's not my work in ecology they fear, but my name. They must believe I'm related—or even a descendant."

"I think they fear you on both counts. My fear is that there might be a nut in the village who'll get hipped on the idea you're a descendant of Sarah Dexter and you're using ecology as an excuse to deprive them of a living."

"And who in the village is regarded as a little less than sane?" I asked pointedly.

"I'm not referring to Miss Mary," he retorted. "Come on. I'll take you back and we'll make another check of the rooms."

"Also the attic. And I do appreciate your company."

His head tilted down until it was a few inches from mine. "I think you're a stubborn idiot. By the same token, I have to admire you—reluctantly."

FOUR

We used my lamp to light our way back to the castle. I asked a few more questions regarding Sarah Dexter. Mr. Randall informed me that the villagers became aware of her powers of witchcraft after the death of her husband. Relatives were informed and came and took her children away. They said that's when she turned to Satan and, according to the legend, became powerful and dangerous.

I asked him then about Mary Selwich. He told me she was the last member of a seafaring family; that her modest cottage gave no evidence of her real wealth, for she owned a large home in Boston, staffed with loyal servants, but she preferred to live on the island. She performed many charitable acts for members of the village, and when young people came here during the summer, unaccompanied by their parents, she took them in and mothered them. In turn, they worshiped her.

"But why have the villagers given her such a cruel nickname?"

"I suppose because she's wealthy and prefers to live modestly. Also, because she has a great understanding and compassion for youth. Many of us haven't the patience to wait until they find themselves. And let's face it, most of them do. Miss Mary, having lived longer than most of us, realizes that."

I made no reply, for I wasn't convinced Miss Mary, as Mr. Randall referred to her, was as innocent as he believed. Also, we were at the house now and I wanted to conduct a thorough inspection of it with him at my side. Though I'd not be driven away, now that I was back in it, the fear which had dissipated, returned, for the house seemed to be filled with a sepulchral quiet.

Mr. Randall lit three more lamps and we each carried two as we moved from room to room on the first floor, then on the second. He searched for a way to the attic, even inspecting the sewing room. While in there, I told him about my first and only encounter with Mary Selwich and the strange costume she was wearing. Also I mentioned that she'd garbed the dummies with costumes from the same era.

"Probably they belonged to Sarah Dexter," he ventured.

"If so, they must be stored in the attic. That's even a better reason for me to inspect it."

"There should be a stairway leading to it."

"There's a door in the butler's pantry downstairs. I was about to check it when the final shriek drove me out of the house."

"We'll check it now."

We returned to the first floor and I noted he moved about the house as if he were quite familiar with it. When he opened the narrow door, there was a cramped corridor leading to a narrow and winding stairway. When he suggested he lead the way, I was more than agreeable. At the top, we paused. The windows were cobwebbed and the odor of dust was prevalent. I moved deeper into it, searching for evidence of an opening of some kind through which a voice could call down, sending an eerie, echoing effect through the house. Mr. Randall was investigating the area on the opposite side.

I had to pause at the far end because several trunks blocked my path, and I called his attention to them. I touched one of the trunks experimentally and lowered one lamp to give it a closer inspection. There wasn't a speck of dust on it. I ran my finger along its surface and held them to the light.

He said, "Looks as if Miss Mary's done a little cleaning up here. I checked two other trunks. They were also spotless."

He set the lamps down, examined the trunks and found them locked. He took some keys from his pocket and tried several. Finally one worked, and the lid of the trunk raised on squeaky hinges.

The delicate scent of lavender came drifting out. I set my lamps down and picked up one of the dresses. It was one which had been draped on the dummy with the childish figure, I told Mr. Randall. Three other dresses lay in there, carefully layered with tissue paper, and they, too, had been on the dummies. But not the one Mary Selwich had worn.

I asked Mr. Randall to open the trunk which set alongside. I settled the garments back carefully, so Miss Selwich wouldn't know they'd been examined. The same key worked on the second trunk. I exclaimed aloud when he raised the lid and saw the beautiful magenta gown. I held it up.

"This is what Miss Mary was wearing."

A frown crossed his brow. "I've seen that before."

"On her?"

"No. I didn't know she dressed up in it."

I reached into the trunk and took out the curled wig she'd worn. "She had this on too."

"Now I know," he said. "The portrait hangs in Mary Selwich's sitting room."

"Of whom?"

"Sarah Dexter."

I regarded the wig and frock. "Do you suppose Mary Selwich believes she is the reincarnation of Sarah Dexter?"

My question amused him. "I doubt it. I think her dressing up is an innocent pastime."

"But why would she have a portrait of a woman who lived over one hundred years ago and whom she couldn't possibly have known?"

He shrugged. "Perhaps she knew the family."

"Even so, she must have taken the portrait from here."

"Not necessarily," he said. "It may have been in her possession."

I wasn't convinced, but made no further comment. I carefully placed the gown back in the trunk, lowered the lid and snapped the lock shut. Mr. Randall did the same with the first one he'd opened.

"I doubt Miss Selwich will know we disturbed the apparel," I said, quite pleased with my efforts.

"Even if she does, I don't think she'll mind," Mr. Randall said complacently.

I spoke as I picked up the lamps. "You don't particularly like me, do you?"

He retrieved his lamps and held one up to view me better. "I like you very much. I just don't like your being so suspicious of Miss Mary."

"I feel I have a good reason to be," I said, leading the way to the stairs. "In any case, Mr. Randall, I'm grateful you came back with me. I hope I won't need to bother you further."

"I hope you will," came the surprising reply. "I think

you need mellowing and I think I'm the man who could do it."

I turned to confront him. "Look, male-chauvinist, if you're trying to rile me, you're wasting your time. I'm quite aware you think me stiff and stodgy, but I shan't let it worry me."

To my surprise, he laughed. "You know, you do sound stiff and stodgy. You even look that way at the moment. I'll see you to your room, then check to determine the doors and windows are secure."

"There's no need for that. I can manage nicely, thank you."

His eyes mocked me. "I'm sure you can. But since this seems to be my night for doing good deeds, I'll perform the chore."

I was too annoyed with him to argue. He knew it and was thoroughly enjoying my discomfiture. I descended the stairs, not pausing until I'd passed through the house and reached the grand stairway. I placed one of the lamps on the table nearby.

"I'll blow it out after I finish checking," he said. "You may go upstairs now. I'll stand here until I hear your door close."

"There's no need. I'm not a child, Mr. Randall."

Again, that mocking smile I found so irritating. "I'm not so sure. Run along. I'll say good night, though I'm sure it's way past the witching hour."

"Good night, Mr. Randall," I replied coldly. I wanted to run up the stairs, but was afraid that in my anger I'd trip and cause him greater amusement.

In my room, I blew out the lamp, but sat on the side of the bed, my ears straining for the sound of his footsteps as he inspected the doors and windows. But he moved quietly and I heard nothing. I moved to the door, cautiously opened it and heard the quiet closing of the front door, followed by the rattle of the knob as he tested

41

it to make certain it was locked. I was grateful a modern latch lock had been installed on it, though I reminded myself it hadn't kept the screamer out. Despite Mr. Randall's denial, I felt certain it had been Miss Selwich or a teenager she'd persuaded to do her bidding. I began to believe the latter more likely, because it would take a strong pair of lungs to make the wild shrill shrieks which had echoed through the castle.

Heedless of the cold, I padded to the window and glanced out. Despite the fact I thought Mr. Randall the rudest man I'd ever encountered, I was relieved to see him pacing in front of the house. I wondered if he intended to stand guard the rest of the night. Though he'd donned a heavy knitted turtleneck sweater before we came here, his hands were thrust deep in his pockets and his shoulders were hunched against the chill night air. My annoyance with him faded, to be replaced with a sense of gratitude. I'd thank him the next time I saw him. He'd probably respond sarcastically, but I'd overlook it. It was the least I could do. I returned to my bed, shivering once again until my body heat had warmed it. I don't know if it was nervous exhaustion or the fact that Mr. Randall was standing guard outside, but I fell asleep immediately and was awakened by sunlight flooding my room.

FIVE

I was grateful for the water heater which allowed me to have a steaming hot shower which I gradually made cooler. If only the electricity was connected, I'd have it made, but I felt certain my work would be completed before the winter really set in. I wore the same outfit as yesterday, for I'd packed only an overnight bag. There'd just not been sufficient room in the car to accommodate my luggage. My laboratory equipment meant far more to me. However, I did bring a pair of knee-high boots, and I tucked my slacks inside.

My breakfast was scanty, for I'd brought little food, knowing I'd return to the village today. My first objective would be to get my luggage. After that, I'd purchase enough groceries so I'd not have to give further thought to it. I'd already made arrangements for ice to be delivered four times a week. There was a large ice box on the back porch which I'd already inspected. It was spotlessly clean and contained only the few food items I'd purchased which needed refrigeration. I continued the work of setting up my laboratory until my watch and the tide schedule informed me I could now walk to the village, high and reasonably dry.

Outside, I surveyed the burned-out shell of my old car. Why did people wish to be so perverse and refuse to accept truths? If biologists, chemists and zoologists like me didn't come up with answers to the problems I was investigating, this would be a deserted village and perhaps an abandoned island before too long. Yet when I'd tried to convince some of the people of that, they laughed at me. Others scowled and muttered under their breaths.

I began my three-mile hike. It was a cool, crisp morning, bright with sunlight and flavored with the perfume of the sea. That was one odor I never wrinkled my nose over. I loved the tang and invigorating freshness of it.

I passed Mr. Randall's cabin and had proceeded about a mile when I came upon another, painted a spanking white and surrounded by a fence, also freshly painted. Late-blooming annuals edged the fence, and I wondered if this might be Mary Selwich's cottage. As I approached it, the door opened and she stood framed in the doorway. Though her attire was not exactly modern, neither was it period. Her black taffeta dress reached to her ankles and was unadorned except for lace collar and cuffs. Her white hair, center-parted and in loose waves, was looped in a coil at her neck.

"Good morning, my dear." Her greeting was as cheery as her smile.

"Good morning, Miss Selwich," I replied.

"I knew you'd be along about now, and I have a pot of coffee ready for us."

"I'm sorry," I said, "but I can't today."

"Yes, you can," she said and opened the door wider.

There was a certain wistfulness in her manner I couldn't resist. I depressed the latch on the gate, pushed it open and walked up the stone path.

"It's kind of you to invite me," I said.

"Kinder of you to accept, my dear."

I'd accepted because I didn't know how to refuse without appearing rude. Though I'd been quite irritated with her yesterday afternoon and even more so last night, it was impossible to feel that way now. Her blue eyes, bearing the innocence of a child, regarded me curiously. The sitting room, flooded with sunshine, was tastefully furnished, but what caught my immediate attention was the portrait over the fireplace.

"It's Sarah Dexter." Miss Selwich closed the door as she spoke. "Papa said she was a rare beauty."

"She certainly was," I agreed.

The portrait breathed with life. The eyes, a luminous brown, seemed to look right through one. The mouth was a little sensuous, the black hair gave off blue lights. I wondered if the women of the village had given her the title of "witch" after the death of her husband, because they feared her breathtaking loveliness.

"This way, my dear."

I guess I'd been almost hypnotized by the portrait. I apologized and followed Miss Selwich into a small dining room. Sparkling china and silver rested on Madeira place mats. A silver coffee urn was already on the table.

"You may pour," she said. "I'll get the coffee cake. It's been out of the oven only minutes. I timed it to coincide with your arrival."

She returned, carrying a silver tray. A large white napkin concealed the coffee cake, but its spicy aroma filled the room, teasing my appetite.

"How did you know I was coming this way?"

She set it down and looked across the table at me. "Do sit down, my dear. Cream or sugar?"

"Neither, thanks."

I must have looked puzzled, for she smiled and said, "I'm a great believer in mental telepathy—or ESP as it's called today."

I ventured a guess. "Perhaps you saw me leave the castle."

"Good gracious, no. My vision isn't that good."

She uncovered the coffee cake and offered it. I took a generous piece. It was almost weightless, even though generously frosted.

"You used binoculars," I speculated.

"I have a pair, but I use them only to look out to sea."

"Then how could you know I was going to the village?"

"I take it you don't believe in a melding of minds even when miles apart."

"I'm a scientist. I require an explanation for everything."

"I suppose life is much less complicated that way."

"I don't agree. I have to find answers. You apparently never have any questions, since you can shut your eyes and see exactly what is happening anywhere you wish."

She nodded. "I saw you and my dear Roger last night. I'm so glad he returned to the castle with you. I only hope you settled the gowns back in the trunks carefully. They're old, you know, and should be handled as gently as a baby."

"You knew we opened the trunks?" I exclaimed.

"Oh yes," she replied placidly. "Do eat your coffee cake, my dear."

I regarded the piece I held. I'd had it halfway to my mouth, but her reply so surprised me, I'd completely forgotten about it. Now I bit into it. It was delicious.

"You do like it," she said, looking pleased. "I can tell by your eyes."

46

"Very much, indeed. I'm glad you invited me in."

"My door will always be open to you. I hope you'll come."

"Mr. Randall told me you have a lovely home in Boston."

"I'm so happy here, I've almost forgotten about it."

"Do you live here alone?"

"Usually. Though from time to time, I have two of my employees come up and go through the place. The castle is another matter. I prefer keeping that up myself. It's what you might call a labor of love."

"Why?"

She gave a dainty shrug of her shoulders. "I think Sarah Dexter would have liked it. I know she's pleased you're living there."

"Mrs. Dexter is long dead. I doubt she'd have any interest in me."

"You could be wrong, you know."

"Why do you say that?"

"Her death was never proven."

"She'd be over one hundred if she were alive today. Unless, of course, you believe, as the islanders do, that she was a witch and witches do not die."

"I believe no such thing. If I lived in Sarah Dexter's time, I'd have probably been called a witch too."

With her powers of perception, I could believe it. I smiled. "May I have another piece of the coffee cake?"

Her blue eyes sparkled with pleasure. "Indeed, yes. My dear Roger enjoys it also." At my look of surprise, she added, "Oh yes, he comes here."

"I was very grateful to have him to go to last night," I said. The opportunity was too good to pass up.

"What happened?" she asked.

"Don't you know?"

"Why should I?" she countered.

47

"But I thought you knew everything that went on here."

She smiled and extended the tray. "Not quite. But I can tell you an easier way to get to the attic."

"By all means, do so."

"The gold-plated candelabra which stand out from the wall over the fireplace in your bedroom. Did you notice them?"

"There's one on each side."

"The one on your right as you face it—just pull it toward you. It opens into the corridor stairway. No need to go down to the butler's pantry."

I thought a moment. "I'll bet you discovered it when you were cleaning the candelabrum."

She gave me a Mona Lisa smile. "I suppose you could say that."

"Or did you know it was there all along?"

Her laughter was light and delicate. She was obviously enjoying my bewilderment.

I finished my coffee cake and licked the sugar from my fingers, determined to enjoy every bit of it. "I thought someone had got in the house last night," I said.

"You mean you thought you heard sounds in the castle?"

"I heard screaming and someone calling to Belial to come."

She sobered. "I've never heard that."

"Or screaming?"

Her head moved slowly from side to side.

"It was horrible. I got up to investigate, but I lost my courage and ran to Mr. Randall's cottage."

"I'm glad he was home. You might have gone mad with fright."

"You honestly don't know anything about it?"

"Not a thing," she replied.

48

"I thought it might have been you," I said. "Or a teenager you befriended."

"They've left the island," she replied. "I sent them home to go back to school."

"But you admitted you tried to frighten me yesterday," I reminded her.

She looked contrite. "It wasn't a nice thing to do and I'm sorry." She arose and started to stack the dishes.

"I'll help," I said.

"No, my dear," she said. "If you want to beat the tide, you must get going. Thank you for coming in."

"Thank you for asking me," I replied. "Please come and visit me."

"I shall," she replied. "When you least expect me." She ignored my look of surprise and led the way to the door. "I'm sorry about what happened to your car."

"Were you still at the castle when it happened? I called to you."

"I couldn't have heard you. My dear Roger's motorbike makes a terrible racket and my hearing isn't all it should be."

I glanced at the portrait over the mantel and wondered how it got there.

As if reading my mind, Miss Selwich said, "I found it in the castle attic. It's too beautiful to be shut away."

"I agree."

"And please don't believe one horrible word you hear about that dear lady." Her voice was almost a plea.

"I shan't," I promised. And I meant it, for there wasn't a trace of evil in that face. "Good-bye, Miss Selwich."

"Please call me Miss Mary. Everyone does—to my face."

I knew what she meant. I said, "Good-bye, Miss Mary."

Once again, I was on my way and I lost no time, for I knew I'd be slowed once I reached the area of tidewater the sea had pulled out. And I was, for the road was nicely muddied. I sank almost over my ankles in the stuff and I gave myself a mental pat I'd had sense enough to don my boots. I was also glad I was young and reasonably fit.

SIX

The village was a conglomeration of houses and little shops, of fish canneries, boatyards and an idle marina. The houses were either red or white, except those the sea air had changed to a dull gray. Streets were narrow, but presented no problem, for there were few cars here. There wasn't anywhere to drive them. Motorcycles and bicycles were sufficient and thriftier to operate, so nobody complained.

The stores might have come out of the nineteenth century, with the general store being a typical example. It was a wood frame building with an open porch and rickety stairs leading up to it, and a double-door entrance. The display windows were about the size of ordinary house windows, but that didn't matter either, because the only things displayed in them were stand-up, cut-out advertising pieces, most of them speckled with age.

Yards were uniformly neat, with their low picket fences and squeaky gates. There were still a few flower gardens in bloom, though at this time of year, even the lawns were turning brown.

The one outstanding structure, representing the only other source of income the village possessed, was the resort hotel. It had been built right after the turn of the century, when it was discovered that rich people from the large cities would pay handsomely for what the islanders accepted as their everyday form of life. It was a large hotel, with more than three hundred rooms. The inside was as properly kept as the outside. Rooms were enormous by present-day standards, and the hotel had been remodeled ten years ago, so that it was modern and efficient.

I wiped my boots on the rubber mat outside the entrance, but I still tracked a little mud into the lobby. I headed straight for the desk where Mr. Perry Tabor, resident manager, was in full charge. The rest of the staff had already gone south for the winter to another hotel.

Mr. Tabor was an islander and stayed in the hotel all winter. He was a spare-looking man, sparsely thatched, red-faced from sun and wind. He wasn't overly friendly and his ways were as set as the granite of the quarries not too far inland.

"So you're back," he greeted me.

"I'm back, Mr. Tabor, and I had to walk."

His lips parted in something resembling a smile. "I thought you'd come running back, Miss Dexter."

"Because of the story regarding Sarah Dexter?"

"She your ancestor?"

"Not that I know of," I replied calmly.

"You know that place you're stayin' is called Witch's Castle?"

"I do."

"Ain't nobody ever stayed there long."

"I signed a three-month lease. If it takes that long to complete my work, I'll live there."

"Why'd you walk back?"

"Because someone attached a fire bomb to my car. It burned down to the framework. I should report it to the mainland police."

"You do that, Miss Dexter. But I'll tell you right now, you won't get much sympathy from those who live here."

"Why not?"

" 'Cause you're takin' their bread and butter away from them, that's why."

"That's not my purpose, though I know some of the islanders who work in factories on the mainland are afraid I'll start some kind of action that will close up the factory and leave them out of work. But if scientists don't find answers to the problems that face the waters around here, the factories might be shut down permanently."

"Don't do no good to tell me."

"Doesn't do any good to tell them either."

"It might if you had a different name."

"Oh, come now, Mr. Tabor. Surely you don't believe in the legend of Sarah Dexter."

"Don't matter much if I do or not," he said.

"I disagree." I decided to attempt flattery. "Certainly a man of your intelligence could do a great deal to convince these people I'm a harmless scientist whose concern is cleaning up the environment—in this case, the ocean. As for the late Sarah Dexter . . ."

"Ain't no evidence she ever died," he butted in.

"She could have drowned in the sea trying to find a refuge," I retorted, finding it more difficult to hold my temper in check. "After all, the story has it that the islanders came with a rope to lynch her—over one hundred years ago."

"They did, but couldn't find hide nor hair of her," he said, looking disappointed at the thought.

53

"I'm glad."

"You're missin' the whole point, Miss Dexter," he said.

I didn't believe I was, but since I still hoped to convince him, I said, "Just what do you mean?"

"Folks here say you got to be a descendant of the witch; otherwise, you'd not have chosen this island."

"What's that got to do with it?" I asked testily.

"You've come back to wreak vengeance on them," he said.

"You must have been watching a silly television series." I softened my words with a smile. "Mr. Tabor, I was born in Pennsylvania. I doubt very much I have a New England ancestor. But since you're so certain I have . . ."

He held up a hand. "I didn't say it. People here did."

I had an idea he did say it—behind my back. "Anyway, I'm going to put through a call to my father. I'll use the desk phone if I may and you can listen in. Just set the phone up for a long-distance call."

For a moment he looked as if he'd refuse. "You'll have to pay for it."

"I intend to."

He went to the switchboard; I dialed direct and had Dad on the phone in less than two minutes.

"I just called to tell you the hotel closed for the winter and I've leased an old house at the tip of the island. I was working at that end anyway, so it's more convenient for me. Just address my mail to General Delivery."

"How's it coming?" Dad asked.

"It's too early to tell yet. I should know something in a few days."

"Made any friends?"

I chuckled. "Everyone's afraid of me."

"What for?"

"They think I'm a descendant of a woman reputed to

54

be a witch, who lived here around a hundred years ago. Her name was Sarah Dexter."

He laughed. "You could be, you know. Your ancestors come from Salem."

"Fine," I said flatly. I glanced over to the switchboard. When Mr. Tabor's eyes met mine, I knew all I'd done was made things more difficult for myself. "Well, there's one thing. I'll have no distractions so far as the islanders are concerned."

"What's wrong?"

"Well, besides the Sarah Dexter thing, they think I'm here to deprive them of a living. I don't know which is worse around here—being descended from a witch or studying marine pollution."

He sobered. "You haven't been threatened, have you?"

I decided not to mention the car, or the screams and voice I heard in the castle. "I haven't been shot at, or beaten up. I don't think they'd go that far."

"I'm sure they wouldn't. As for your ancestors, your grandfather was born in Philadelphia and so was I."

"And before that?" I prodded.

"Why worry about it?"

"I'm not worried," I said. "It's just that I've leased the house once owned by Sarah Dexter who, incidentally, was a beautiful lady."

"How do you know?"

"I saw her portrait."

"Did she have a dimple in one cheek?" he teased.

"I didn't notice. The next time I'll look more carefully."

"You do that. And keep in touch."

"Thanks, Dad. Give my love to Mother."

"I'll do that. If I can help in any way, just give me a ring."

"I will," I promised and hung up.

Mr. Tabor returned to the desk. "Isn't Salem where

all the witches were bred? Where most executions for witchcraft took place?"

"It was, Mr. Tabor."

"Then you could be a direct descendant of Sarah Dexter. You should've asked your pa to check it."

"The next time I phone him, I will," I said flatly. "Now, if you don't mind, I'll get my luggage."

He pointed a bony finger at the door next to the stairway. "There, in that closet. I brought them downstairs after you left. We're closing up the rooms for the winter."

I went to the closet and picked up the heaviest of the three pieces. I'd take that to the boat first. I knew better than to try to hire someone to carry them for me.

Mr. Tabor called to me as I was going out the door. "You goin' straight back, Miss Dexter?"

I set down the bag. "Why?"

"Mail's due in an hour. I'll see you get it if you're still in town."

"I'm going to shop for groceries and then see Mr. Abrams."

"Canceling your lease already?"

"No," I said firmly.

"Just as well. He wouldn't let you out of it. He may not be at his tackle shop. Maybe I could help."

It was as good a way as any of finding out what my business with Mr. Abrams was. I said, "I want the electricity turned on. The house is wired."

"The wires been down now for maybe a year or so. Nobody ever bothered to put 'em up again. Tourists who like the place—before they spend a night in it—all want to live primitively. To my mind, they're crazy."

I made him no answer. I knew that the moment the lobby door closed on me, he'd be on the phone, verbally publicizing the fact that I was probably Sarah Dexter's great-great granddaughter—if not Sarah Dexter herself.

I lugged my bag to the marina where my boat,

56

fortunately, was riding safely. That is, if nobody had hidden a fire bomb aboard. I'd check that before starting out.

Before I returned to the hotel for the other luggage, I visited the general store and made some rather extensive purchases of food and supplies. They were to be delivered to my boat in exactly one hour, I told the shopkeeper, and that's when they'd be paid for. I wasn't going to pay for them and then be told to get them there as best I could.

I found Mr. Abrams in his store. He was the personification of a dour New Englander, a type the old movies liked to depict: tall, angular, taciturn, balding, with icy blue eyes that had faded from constant exposure to the sun.

"Good morning, Mr. Abrams."

"Afternoon." He said it, not as a greeting, but as a statement of correction. I automatically glanced at my watch. He was right.

"I've come about having the electricity turned on. I don't think that's too much to ask, and if it's not too expensive, I'm willing to pay for it myself."

"Can't do it," he said.

"Why not?"

"Place just bought by new owner. Sold it the day after you signed the lease."

"Now see here," I exclaimed, "you're not putting me out. The lease is valid . . ."

"Didn't say it wasn't."

"But the new owner . . . ?"

"Knows you're in there and all right with him. He's from Boston. If you want improvements, you talk to him."

"I have to reach him in Boston?"

"Ah-yah."

"I suppose he wants the place to retain its quaintness." I knew from his smug look that I was right.

"Can't blame him for that," came the caustic comment. "Another thing. Boy that delivers ice to Witch's Castle, won't deliver to you."

"Why not?"

" 'Cause of your name, that's why not."

I walked out before I lost my temper. I retrieved the rest of my luggage, took it to the boat and waited for the groceries to be delivered. I settled for them, started the engine and cruised away from the dock before I headed out and opened her up. Not until the fast little craft was roaring full speed, did I remember about fire bombs. I kept going. —

SEVEN

I tied up the boat at the rickety little pier, transferred my luggage and groceries to it and made five trips to the castle. I brought my luggage upstairs, then decided to unpack later. I was eager to get back to my lab work, for it was only mid-afternoon. I returned to the kitchen and gathered up my string of specially prepared plates, attached to a rope with an anchor at the bottom. I would lower these plates, set to rest in the ocean at various prearranged depths with the anchor holding the line to the bottom. The plates would collect protozoa, barnacles and sea worms which could then be examined.

I knew exactly where I wanted to plant this trap, and I sent the motorboat directly to that spot, opposite a huge pipe that was spilling waste material from one of the factories into the sea.

I lowered the trap, saw that the buoy was intact, and

then I began to back off from the location. As I did so, I was facing the island and I saw two flashes of light, as if from a mirror. I stopped the boat and let it drift until I knew what had caused those flashes. Someone was watching me through binoculars.

I pointed the prow of the boat straight in the direction from which the flashes came and I opened her wide. It eased my anger and frustrations to go skimming at top speed over the water and gave me a sense of power that I didn't feel on land.

When I was close to the shore and saw no one, I turned my attention back to my work. A third of a mile off the island tip, I stopped the boat again. This time, I began another method of testing the island waters. I used a plankton sampler, a device which could be lowered to any desired depth. A sterile bottle under vacuum would open, and sea water at this particular depth would flow into it. I took three samples before I returned to the pier.

I had just reached the castle when Mr. Randall hailed me. I placed the water-filled bottles and the apparatus on the porch and sat down on the steps.

He sat down beside me and indicated the sampler apparatus. "Funny-looking tackle."

"I set out some traps," I said, "and then I took samples of island water. I want to check on the plankton. I presume you know what they are."

He nodded. "Life in the sea."

"If there were no plankton, there'd be no fish. Trouble is, the plankton are plentiful, but they're also contaminated. Small fish life eat them, bigger fish life eat the smaller fish life, and it goes right on up the scale to a point where the last fish to enjoy a meal is hooked or netted and provides a meal for a human. If all the ocean life eaten on the way up that ecological scale are contaminated with DDT, phosphates, heavy metals or any of the countless contaminants that are thrown into our

60

oceans, then the big fish providing the meal is also poisoned, and so will be the human who eats that fish. Provided he eats enough of them."

I stopped suddenly, embarrassed I'd been so carried away by the subject.

"Go on," he urged. "Tell me more."

I regarded him with surprise. "Are you serious?"

"Completely."

It was all the encouragement I needed to warm to my subject. "Oyster beds are growing smaller, lobsters are not as plentiful as they should be. Clams die at an early age. The islanders depend to a great extent on what's taken out of the sea. If it's poisoned and people find out, there won't be any call for it."

"Right," he said. "That's why they'd like to transfer you to some remote spot, probably south of Pago Pago. If their business is destroyed by your studies, you'll be the one they'll hold responsible."

I looked skeptical. "If anybody important reads my thesis."

"Send a copy to HEW in Washington," he suggested. "Put a *TOP SECRET, EYES ONLY* stamp on it and it'll be read. Other than that, what have you been doing?"

"I've had a busy day. I headed for the village this morning. Miss Mary intercepted me and invited me in for coffee and coffee cake. Very delicious."

"Now that you got better acquainted, can you imagine that gentle lady calling on Belial in an effort to frighten you?"

I smiled. "Frankly, no. But she does puzzle me."

"In what way?"

"She knew I was frightened last night. She knew we searched the attic and inspected the gowns. She even told me how I could get up there from the second floor."

"How?" he asked.

"Don't you know?"

61

I must have betrayed my skepticism because he said, "Believe me, Miss Dexter, I do not."

"A candelabrum in my bedroom over the fireplace is pulled forward and a portion of wall opens."

"Did you check it?"

"Not yet. I'd really forgotten about it."

"I wonder how she knew," he said.

"I suggested she must have discovered it when she was dusting. She only smiled mysteriously. I wonder why she's taken such a liking to this place."

"Probably the liking is for Sarah Dexter."

"You mean the mental anguish she must have suffered because of the bigotry of the villagers."

He nodded. "Miss Mary has a great talent for compassion."

"She also has a talent for knowing what's happening to others and what their plans are. At least, I didn't tell anyone—not even you—I was going into the village this morning."

"Even if you had, I haven't seen Miss Mary today."

"Yet she knew I was going to the village. She'd even timed the coffee cake to be ready just before I reached her cottage. The coffee, freshly perked, set on the dining room table."

"ESP?" he suggested.

"*She* said so," I replied. "But I'm a scientist."

"Yet you did like Miss Mary." He made it a statement.

"Tremendously. I also saw the portrait of Sarah Dexter. She was beautiful."

"Very."

"I called my Dad from the village and learned some rather unsettling news. His ancestors came from Salem."

He grunted. "That's all you need. Just hope the villagers don't hear about it. They'll be more certain than ever now you came to get revenge on them."

"I'm sure they know about it. I made the call in the

presence of Mr. Tabor in the hope that I could convince him to persuade the villagers I was completely unconnected with Sarah Dexter."

Mr. Randall smiled. "So long as he wasn't listening in."

"But he was. I invited him to do so."

"You've got problems, girl."

"Don't I know it. Well, I'll just have to cope with it as best I can. This wasn't what I'd call one of my better days."

"More problems?"

"The castle has been sold to somebody from Boston who purchased it for its quaintness and therefore would not want the electricity connected. How do I work without it? Leeuwenhoek may have used only candles for light, but with my instruments, it won't work."

"You can't make them raise the fallen light poles and wires because you leased the place as is. On the other hand, what's to stop you from running some wires here? Say from my place. It's not too far. A couple of poles would do it, and I know where they are. Also, the wire."

"Can it be done?" I asked.

"My stint in Vietnam was with the engineers, and we learned how to do a lot of things no sane engineer, safe in this country, would think of. I can rig the line. The juice will go through my meter, but I'm sure we can come to terms about sharing the bill."

"Mr. Randall, you have no idea how grateful I'd be if you did this."

He nodded. "We might even have ourselves a lobster and clam cookout on the beach some day soon."

"It sounds good."

His smile was one of boyish enthusiasm. "Tomorrow?"

"I'll be too busy."

"Think about it," he urged. "A beach party. I bury a keg in the sand over a fire that has heated stones. Into the keg I put a layer of seaweed, a layer of lobster, more

63

seaweed, a layer of clams. And soon there's enough for six or eight people, which is just about the amount two people will eat."

"It sounds delightful, but not tomorrow." I stood up. "You'll have to excuse me now. I want to check these samples while there's still sunlight, so I can get a reasonable amount of use from my microscope."

He stood up and helped me gather my samples. "Good luck. By that, I mean I hope you don't find what you're looking for."

"So do I," I said. "For the sake of the villagers and all mankind."

"I'll stop by tomorrow to learn the results of your test. I know better than to invite you over for dinner tonight."

I smiled my thanks. "I'll take a rain check on it."

I went inside, eager to study the samples. Sea life won't live too long after being trapped, and my work was important. Much more important than a beach cookout, I decided.

I moved a table closer to a window with light mainly from the west. There I placed my microscope and the samples of sea water. I prepared for an examination of live microscopic sea life, using well slides over which I carefully placed fragile cover slips. I had to adjust the mirror, for I hadn't used one in a long time, as I preferred artificial illumination because it was brighter. I brought down the medium lens, got the drop of water into focus, and at once I noticed the complete lack of oyster and clam larvae. These are minute and fragile—about the size of a grain of wheat.

Usually, the waters close to the surface teem with them, for they feed on the plant life of the plankton. When they are not in evidence, something is wrong with the ecology of the water. The answer was simple to find. The plankton on which these larvae fed was as missing as they were. If the larvae found no food, they died. The plankton was not there because something had killed it and now there'd be far fewer oysters and clams for the island people to harvest. This was an important, though not unexpected find, and I made detailed entries in my notebooks. I would now have to take samples of sea water close to the drains pouring wastes into the ocean. The cause of the disappearance of the larvae and its food could be one of several chemicals, and I anticipated no trouble in determining exactly which one it was.

I sat back, frustrated by making this find and being able to do nothing more about it than writing the figures in a notebook. I made up my mind then, that when my work was well on the way and I had enough facts to warrant the action, I'd send a report to the Federal Waterquality Administration. Maybe they'd do something.

A stomach growl informed me that my last nourishment had been with Miss Mary at mid-morning, and now the sun was already going down. I finished my note-taking, then I walked the dozen steps from the laboratory to the kitchen cabinets and the range, for everything was in the same room.

I opened a can of soup, heated it and ate it along with some of the fresh biscuits I'd bought in the village. It wasn't an exciting meal, but it didn't matter because I was too intent on my work to care much about food. I washed and dried my dishes, took off my rubber lab apron which doubled nicely for use in the kitchen. I walked through the house to the library. I took a pack of matches from my pocket, struck one and touched it to a fat candle with a double wick which set on the desk. I seated myself in a leather chair, propped my feet on the matching ottoman and let myself go limp.

EIGHT

It had been a busy day and I was pleasantly exhausted. Slowly the thought came to me that, at the moment, I didn't feel like a dedicated scientist, but rather like a companionless girl, suddenly aware of the loneliness of the castle. I recalled last night with a shudder. That scream had seemed to come from the depths of hell. Reason told me it had not, yet it had sent me fleeing into the night, straight to Mr. Randall. I smiled as I recalled Miss Mary referring to him as "my dear Roger." Apparently, she was quite taken with him.

I thought of poor Sarah Dexter, who was so beautiful and so hated by the villagers of one hundred years ago, and wondered if I were really a descendant. I also wondered if Papa didn't really know. It would seem that such a story would be handed down from generation to generation. Or, in those days, would it have been suppressed? I recalled Mr. Randall telling me that Sarah Dexter's children had been taken from her after the death of her husband. Why had she allowed it? Perhaps she thought they'd be safer away from here. A mob, led on by a bigot, could be persuaded to commit horrible deeds.

I chided myself for dwelling on what had happened one hundred years ago. I knew I wouldn't have, except that for the terror I'd been subjected to last night.

Even then, my common sense told me the scream and voice I'd heard had been that of a human. The idea was to drive me from this castle. Nonetheless, I realized what a comfort a telephone could be—and a car. Also, electricity. Should I be frightened again, I couldn't run to Mr. Randall for help. He'd think me a silly schoolgirl—or worse, that I was infatuated with him.

The yellow candle flame seemed to mock me. I wondered how it would feel to be the descendant of a reputed witch. The idea held little appeal to me. I suppose the reason I didn't ask Dad if I were a descendant of Sarah Dexter was twofold: Surprise had robbed me of curiosity, and also, Mr. Tabor was listening in on our conversation.

I smiled at my foolishness. What if my ancestors were from Salem? There was no such thing as a witch. Those unfortunate individuals who were imprisoned or put to death were punished either through ignorance or viciousness. I pushed the footstool aside and got up. I had to carry the large candelabrum into the kitchen with me, for the castle was now in darkness except for the two lamps I'd left lit at my laboratory table. The book about sea plankton was on my lab table. I placed a pad and pen inside the science book, tucked it under my arm, picked up one lamp and returned to the library. It would give sufficient light when placed on the table alongside the easy chair. Yet when I settled myself again, the lamp threw eerie and menacing shadows. I opened my book to the desired page and began to read.

I succeeded in checking and rechecking information about the effect of mercury and pesticides in ocean larvae, and everything confirmed what I suspected. Somewhere, along or above the channel, poisons were being dumped into the water. It it was not stopped, the oyster beds would die, crabs and lobsters would either perish or swim to safer waters. How could I convince villagers who were trying to prevent me from gaining this information which concerned them more than anyone in the world, that my purpose was to benefit them?

I expanded some entries, making a first-draft outline. The actual writing of the formal thesis would come later, when everything was assembled, but I felt that I was making a good start.

Outside, I could hear a wind coming up. I knew they sometimes sweep in from the sea quickly and are often a portent of cold weather on the way. I paid little attention to it, being so engrossed in my work. But something unpleasant was intruding on my concentration. I raised my head finally and sniffed. Gradually, so that I was only half aware of it, a sharp, strange odor had been slowly filling the library, probably the entire castle. I got up hastily. I was certain I'd left no chemicals where there might have been an accident. In fact, no combination of chemicals that I had, or knew of, could have created this smell. It was as if someone had dug up an old carcass and was boiling it.

I'd left nothing cooking on the range. I picked up the lamp and hurried into the kitchen. On the range—and large enough to cover two burners—was a black kettle. I'd noticed it in one of the cupboards, but gave no heed to it because I'd surely never need a cooking pot like that. Now it was giving off a cloud of steam as it boiled vigorously, emitting the vilest smell I'd encountered in a long time.

I hastily pulled the heavy pot off the burners, almost burning my hands in doing so. I picked up a lamp and held it so I could look into the pot with its swirling mess of rank substances.

I took a long fork from one drawer and thrust it into the mixture. I speared something and lifted it out of the water. It seemed to be made of bones and feathers. I held the lamp closer and discovered I was holding the body of a bird.

I hastily and disgustedly dropped it back into the pot. I couldn't find any pot holders, so I settled for a large terry towel, which I wadded and wrapped around the handle of the pot.

Trying to keep from gagging, I carried it outside and ran with it for about a hundred yards before I set it down and tilted the pot so that the contents spilled onto the ground.

Who had done it, and why? Getting into the castle wouldn't have been difficult; it had been vacant most of the day. The mixture could have been prepared elsewhere after the pot had been stolen. Whoever had placed it on the range, had done so while I was in the library, engrossed in my work. It was a simple matter to carry the pot in, place it on the range, light the burners, then make a quiet exit.

I thought of a witch's brew, allegedly made up of all sorts of things like toads, snakes and, in some instances, birds. I recalled fairy tales of wicked witches who brewed such concoctions, but the whole thing was so absurd that I couldn't reconcile it to our modern world.

I left the back door open and went through the house to open the front door. The place needed airing to dispel the foul odor which had permeated the entire first floor.

However, I had to hold fast to the front door, bracing it with my body, for the wind was now raging with such force that to open the door wide would be like having a tornado blow through. I stood there until I was thoroughly chilled, then forced the door shut. I lost no time going back to the kitchen to shut and bolt that door, for a heavy rumble of thunder warned of an approaching storm.

Too unnerved by what I'd found in the kitchen to resume my work, I stood irresolutely for a moment. I knew better than to think the horrible concoction had been conjured up by a supernatural force. Obviously, it had been done to further frighten me—which it had—but I would still not leave the castle or the island. No one was going to frighten me away from the project I was engaged in and intended to complete. I checked the shelf where I'd seen a large black pot: It was missing.

I put out one lamp and carried the other into the hall. I remembered then that the candle was still lit in the library. As I headed for it, the door started to move slowly and creakily, attesting to rusting hinges. It finally closed, but light from the candle slipped beneath the door. I bit at my lower lip to steady myself. I had to go into that room. I didn't know if anyone was there, but if so, I decided I might as well find out.

Just as I took a step, the floor moved under my feet. It was a distinct movement of the *house*—not similar to the sharp jolt of an earthquake. I knew what that was like, having visited California. This seemed as if a pair of giant hands grasped the house and slowly rocked it, with the earth not involved in any way.

There was a crash of glass behind the closed door. I recalled a large cut-glass vase on a round table to one side of the fireplace, the hearth of which was marble. I walked resolutely to the door, gripped the knob and turned it.

71

The candle still burned brightly, its flame steady. I glanced around; no one was there. But the table which had held the vase was empty. I went further into the room. The vase, shattered to bits, lay on the hearth. I returned to the kitchen for a broom and dustpan.

I set the lamp on the floor and carefully swept the glass into a heap. When I started to sweep the pieces of glass onto the dustpan, the lamp was in my way; I picked it up and was about to set it on the table when it began to move away from me. I was startled but determined and reached out for it, attributing its movement to the rocking of the house, though that had now stopped. My hand had just touched the surface of the table, when it moved further away. It was a slow movement, but a definite one. Stunned, I watched it continue on its course until it was at least two feet from me.

The wick of the candle and that of the lamp started to flicker wildly. At the same time, the heavens seemed to open and torrents of rain slapped down on the house. The candle went out.

I waited no longer. I had to get out, and I knew I'd go to the one person with whom I'd feel secure—Roger Randall. I almost ran to the front door, and the moment I opened it, the wind pulled it from my grasp and flung it wide.

I made no attempt to close it, but ran across the porch, down the steps and headed for Mr. Randall's house. I was soaked before I'd taken ten steps and I was battered now by heavy rain and hailstones which stung as they hit my face.

I fell three times on my way to the cottage, and I couldn't keep a straight course, for the wind tossed me about as if I were a dried leaf. I'd lost the lamp on my first fall, and only a sharp bolt of lightning revealed the cottage. As before, welcoming light flowed through the window. I stumbled and weaved my way forward. I was soaked to the skin and I was shivering from the cold, but I had one thought—to get to the cottage. There I'd find shelter and comfort.

NINE

I called his name over and over as my open palms pounded the door. There was no reply. My hand slid down the wet door to the knob. I turned it, but the door was locked. I moaned aloud in desperation. There was no other place for me to go except Miss Mary's, and I'd never find my way there. I couldn't see through the rain, which still fell in torrents. The porch was no shelter, for the wind was driving that way and the water now poured off me. I felt weighted down by my clothes, which could absorb no more moisture.

I pounded on the door again, but not with the same force, for I was growing exhausted. My breathing was still labored from the effort it had taken to get here.

Then I heard something behind me and I turned swiftly. A figure loomed before me, blocking my path. I screamed.

"Gale!" It was Roger Randall.

"Thank God," I exclaimed.

His arms enclosed me and I pressed my head against the wetness of his jacket.

"What are you doing here?" he asked.

"I was frightened," I said. I was shivering so violently, my teeth chattered as I spoke.

"You can tell me about it inside. You've got to get out of those clothes."

He had the key in the lock and the door opened before he finished speaking. He led me to the fireplace where papers and kindling were already laid. He touched a match to it, put on smaller logs until the flame caught.

"Stay there," he said. "I'll bring you some towels and a robe so you can get out of those clothes."

He returned and set the towels and robe on the footstool which he'd pushed before the fireplace. The kindling had already caught and was sending out welcoming warmth.

"I have to change too," he said. "Call out when I can come back."

"What will I do with these soaking things I take off?"

"Put them in the kitchen sink. My bedroom is off the kitchen. I'll stay there until you call my name. And make it Rog."

"Thanks," I said gratefully.

He left me then and I removed my sodden garments. I doubted they'd be of any value again. I toweled myself dry, donned his robe and padded in my bare feet to the kitchen, placing everything in the sink, except for my boots. I could wear them back, for they fitted snugly and the moisture hadn't got into them. I set them far enough away from the fireplace so that the leather wouldn't stiffen, but near enough so they could absorb a little warmth.

I couldn't seem to stop shivering. I called out to Rog.

He appeared, dressed in sweater, slacks and moccasins.

"I'll put on some coffee and spike it with a little brandy," he said. "We can both use it. Get back to that fire."

I didn't argue, for I was really chilled. I resumed my seat by the fire and pressed a dry towel against my head, for my hair was still dripping. Though cut short all over, it was thick and still very wet.

He came in then, placed two larger logs on the fire and took the towel from me. He felt my hands, then my feet. "You really got a chill," he said. "Sit facing the fire. I'll dry your hair. You're not to say a word until I bring you coffee."

I didn't protest, for I knew it would do no good. He gave orders and expected them to be obeyed. Tonight, knowing it was for my well-being, I didn't even mind. He patted the excess moisture from my hair, then rubbed it briskly until it was dry.

"I forgot to bring a comb," he said.

"I can finger-comb it," I said and did so.

He dropped the towel onto the hearth and squatted down beside me. "Feeling better?"

"Much," I said. "I think my feet are toasting."

"Let them," he said, smiling. "For a little while, I thought you were headed for a case of galloping pneumonia. I'll get the coffee."

He returned with two mugs, handing me one. The mingled aroma of brandy and coffee was stimulating.

"Are you warmed enough now to sit in the leather chair?" he asked.

"Yes."

"Good. I'll take the footstool."

We seated ourselves, but he left the room and returned with an afghan which he spread over my lap, wrapping my feet in it.

I smiled and thanked him. "I feel so safe and secure

here, it almost seems embarrassing to tell you why I came."

"I'm glad you came, but I know something frightened you to make you come."

"It did," I admitted. "And it sounds fantastic."

"Tell me anyway. But first, take a few sips of your coffee."

Again I obeyed, cupping my hands around the mug, enjoying its warmth. Then I related, in detail, what had happened—from finding the foul brew stewing on the range, to the table which moved when I attempted to place the lamp on it. He asked no questions, made no comment until I'd completed my story.

"Do you know if anyone else was in the house?"

"I heard nothing, but someone must have come into the kitchen when I was in the library. I know the back door wasn't locked. I also know the horrible brew was stewed in a black kettle which I'd noticed yesterday on a low shelf in the pantry. It's missing."

"There's no question but someone wants you out of the castle."

I grimaced. "If I only knew who."

"I know who did not put the kettle of brew on the stove," he said.

"Who?"

"Miss Mary. After I left you, I went directly to her cottage to invite her to come back and have dinner with me. Though she does a great deal of walking, she has a little car which she drives about. I told her I'd drive her here and bring her home. Instead, she insisted I have dinner at her house."

"I'm sure it was delicious."

"It was. She's an excellent cook."

"She makes the best coffee cake I've ever tasted."

He smiled. "I'm jealous. I thought she made it just for me."

"Then I feel honored," I said. "I know she's very fond of you."

"I'm fond of her," he said.

"She even refers to you as 'my dear Roger.'"

"To my face, also," he said, laughing. "I like it."

"You merit it," I replied, returning the smile. "I'm ashamed I ever suspected her."

"Well, now." He switched his gaze to the fire and regarded the half-burned logs thoughtfully. "I don't mean to imply she isn't shrewd or clever and maybe a bit sly. She has a way of getting around you—making you think you're doing something special for her, when all the time it was in her mind to have you do exactly that."

I laughed. "And she believes in a melding of minds—ESP."

"Don't laugh." He got up and sat down in a chair to one side of the fireplace. "We were about to have coffee when she got my coat and told me to get right back to the cottage."

I sobered. "Do you think she knew someone was up to mischief?"

"I wouldn't say that. I'm sure if she knew," he spoke slowly, as if seeking the proper choice of words, "she'd have been at the castle to warn you before it happened. But it could be your terror was transmitted to her."

"I do like her and I can understand your fondness for her, but she puzzles me. I can't help but think she is, in some way, connected with what's happening at the castle."

"Perhaps her only connection is to see that nothing happens to you," he reasoned.

"I'm sure she wishes me no harm. But perhaps her real sympathies are with the villagers. After all, you said she was very compassionate."

"She is," he replied firmly. "And you know what the villagers call her. Not all of them, of course. But Miss

79

Mary is an individualist. She has a mind of her own and her opinions rarely coincide with those of the villagers. That's why they've given her that cruel nickname." His head moved from side to side. "No. I can't believe she's in cahoots with the villagers—if it is the villagers who are behind this harrassment of you."

"Who else?" I asked.

"I don't know."

"You're not thinking of that foolish witch story—or that I'm a descendant of Sarah Dexter, I hope."

"Maybe I am."

"You believe in the supernatural?" I exclaimed.

"No, no, no. I just think someone wants you out of that castle and it might not be the villagers."

"Who, then?"

"That's what I'm going to try to figure." His head tilted in a listening attitude. "I believe the rain's stopped. You look beat. You may have my bedroom. I can sleep well in the chair you're sitting in and the footstool."

"Oh no," I replied, standing up so quickly, I forgot my feet were wrapped in the afghan and would have taken a header had he not jumped up and caught me.

He said, with a half smile, "Believe me, Gale, you'll be quite safe here."

I bent over to untangle my feet, wanting to hide my embarrassment. "I know that. It's just that my lab equipment is at the castle and I'm afraid someone may get in and wreck it."

"Suppose you were there alone," he said. "You couldn't prevent it from being destroyed if someone was bent on doing just that."

"But at least I could try."

"Even now, it might be smashed to bits."

I sobered, knowing he spoke the truth. "I ran like a coward. Twice. I don't blame you for laughing at me."

His hand left my waist and tilted my chin upward. "I'm

80

not laughing at you. You're not a coward. You're an intelligent, dedicated young woman for whom I have tremendous respect. I'm also developing a growing concern for your safety and well-being. And for a very good reason."

His eyes were regarding me with a great deal of warmth and he was holding me so close I could feel his quickening heartbeat. His head bent forward and he kissed me. Not a long, ardent kiss, or a fiery, passionate embrace. It was a gentle kiss, yet when our lips touched, I felt my pulse leap and I became annoyed with myself. I didn't want to become involved with Roger Randall or any man. I had a job to do, and nothing or no one was going to interfere with it.

I placed my hands against his chest and pushed him away. "Please. "You've been very kind. Don't spoil it."

He released me immediately. "I'm sorry. May I still call you Gale—or do you prefer Miss Dexter?"

"I want you to call me Gale—I want us to be friends —but that's all. Just friends."

He stepped back. "I'll do my best. Now I'll get you some of my clothes and bring you back to the castle."

He left the room and I untangled my feet from the afghan, folded it and placed it across the back of the chair. He returned then with some cotton velour lounging slacks which tied at the waist with a thick cord. Over it went a matching top. He also brought some long hose.

"Put them on. I have an all-weather coat I'll get for you. How are your boots?"

"Fine. They fit snugly, so they didn't get wet inside."

I dressed and he returned with the coat, holding it for me to slip my arms into.

He said, "I'm going back to the castle with you and check the rooms while you check your equipment."

I sensed his rebuff and felt I merited it. But there was no visible evidence he'd been hurt, and I thought perhaps

81

I was flattering myself that his interest in me was very great. Regardless, I couldn't help but steal a final glance back into the room when he opened the door. I remembered how grateful I'd been to see him and how he'd taken over.

"Forget something?"

His question startled me. "Oh no. I just want to thank you for being so kind."

He looked amused. "Call on me anytime. I'm in the classified."

He laughed then and I joined him. The tension was broken. We went out into the night. There was no further evidence of the storm other than the intermittent dripping of water from trees and shrubbery we passed. The road, of course, was still muddy, but that was a minor inconvenience.

At the castle, he checked the rooms on the first and second floor. He also asked to see the entrance which led from my bedroom to the attic. I led the way and pointed out the candelabrum on the right of the fireplace. He pulled it forward and a paneling on the wall near my bed opened. He carried a lamp into the opening.

"I'm going to close it and see if I can open it from in here. If I don't come out in one minute, pull on the candelabrum."

As he moved the panel, I watched the candelabrum go back into place. I went over and examined the section carefully, but it had been so cleverly constructed, I could see no evidence of the separated wood. I heard him pounding experimentally on the wall, though the sound was muffled and seemed to come from a great distance. When a minute passed and he didn't open it, I went to the fireplace, stood on tiptoe and pulled the candelabrum down. The panel swung open and he stepped out.

"No way of opening it from the other side. You can't even see a separation in the wood."

"You can't on this side either."

He held his lamp close to the wall, examined it carefully, then turned to me.

"Tomorrow, I'm going to string wires from my place so you'll have electricity. You can't be living in this place without it."

"I think I'll have a lot more courage with it."

"You have courage," he said quietly. "But whether you like it or not, I'm remaining downstairs tonight. In the library, to see if there's a repeat of what happened."

"Thanks, Rog," I said. "I'm always thanking you and doing nothing in return for your kindness."

"It's my pleasure," he said, smiling. "I'll probably be gone before you get up, but I'll stay until daylight. Don't be frightened if you hear sounds. I'll be prowling. I'll even clean up the mess of glass on the hearth."

"Please don't. It will keep."

"Go to bed and get some rest. You look beat."

"I am. It's been quite a day."

I closed the door after him, undressed and got into my nightgown. My sigh as I got into bed was not so much of weariness as relief that Rog Randall would be downstairs. At the same time, I knew I had to stop running to him for help. Otherwise, I'd become involved. He had tremendous masculine appeal, was gentle and kind, and I liked the firm, resonant tone of his voice. I liked everything about Rog Randall and I'd be forever grateful to him for all . . .

I caught myself up short. I'd thought about him enough. I was a scientist and I had no time for a foolish romance which might lead to the altar. Or would it, I wondered. Was it just the circumstances which had brought on the intimacy of the moment? I'd not waste another thought on it, yet I couldn't help but give a grudging wonder as to what was going through Roger Randall's mind at this moment.

I forced myself to think of my work and how lucky I

was that my laboratory was still intact . . . eventually, I drifted off to sleep. I didn't even remember until the following morning that I hadn't unpacked.

TEN

I wakened to bright sunlight. The heavy pounding of the surf, plus the brisk wind which whistled through my window, was the only evidence of the heavy rains of the previous night. I made my bed, got my luggage from the closet and unpacked. I'd brought practical things, mostly —slacks suits and sweaters. However, I had also packed a green and gray woolen plaid ankle-length skirt, with matching stole and a green satin blouse, high-necked and long-sleeved. I'd yet to wear it, but it looked both quaint and elegant.

Suddenly, I hoped an opportunity to dress up would present itself. As for now, I selected a dark green pants and tunic outfit and tied a green print scarf around my head. Downstairs, I looked in the library. Rog wasn't there, but then, I hadn't expected he would be. The broken heap of glass had been swept up; the broom and dustpan returned to the kitchen.

I made instant coffee and nibbled on a couple of crackers. My attention was drawn to a note, propped up on my lab desk. It was from Rog.

Dear Gale,

The night passed uneventfully. Just after dawn, I went outside and saw the kettle, still tipped on its side, and beyond it, the carcasses of birds. Just wanted you to know I believe your story. Also, I'd like to get my hands on the sadist responsible.

Do take care. I'll keep an eye on the castle, and as for you—be on guard.

Rog

I was a little disappointed with the casual tone of the message, but I told myself it was what I wanted. I started to put the note in my jacket pocket, then decided to burn it, lest it slip out and fall into the wrong hands. I touched a match to one corner of the paper. When it was almost consumed, I dropped it in the sink, then turned my attention to my work. The traps I'd set had not been out very long, but if my guess was right, there'd be sufficient sea life adhering to them, so I could make a better test for the presence of mercury. I deemed that to be the most important hazard, so I would concentrate on it for the time being. If my theories proved to be correct, I was going to contact someone in authority and have something done about the harvest taken from the channel.

When I went outside, I looked for Roger, but he was nowhere to be seen. I judged he was now getting some necessary sleep. I made my way to the rickety pier and found my boat safe, though it had shipped a little water after the storm. I bailed that and mopped up what was left.

I got the engine humming, pushed away from the pier and headed out to the channel. With the wind in my face,

86

the warmth of the sun on my back, I felt as if I could face anything. I spotted the colored buoy I'd set out, hauled up the line and removed the plates. I fastened new ones in their place and lowered the trap again.

Next, I sent the boat into the channel close to the mainland and the spot where a huge pipe was pouring waste into the water. It came out of the pipe with great force, causing the sea to boil. The water around the pipe was a mud red.

I lowered one of my ZoBell bottles with its bent glass tubing, etched to break easily when the messenger weight dropped down the line. When it was at a depth I judged proper, I released the messenger, waited for the bottle to fill up as the water was sucked into it to displace the vacuum. Then I hauled up the bottle. I took two more similar samples above and below the waste pipe before I decided I had a day's work to examine.

I headed straight back toward the pier. Nearing it, I was completely at ease, planning in my mind how I'd run these tests, when something hit the side of the boat, splintering off a small bit of wood that hit my cheek. I raised my hand to the injury. It was wet. My fingers were smeared with blood. I pressed a folded handkerchief against it, wondering just what had happened. There'd been no sound, nobody was in the channel, not another boat was in sight. I was still puzzled when I heard a whining noise just to my right and I saw a little geyser spring up on the surface of the calm sea. Then I knew— I was being shot at.

I gave the wheel a hard turn to starboard, gunned the craft to its fullest and as I retreated from the shoreline, I zigged the boat to keep from being hit. At a safer distance I slowed, stood up and looked back. I could see no one, yet somebody on shore had shot at me and I was positive the shooting came from near the private pier I was using. There was a good fringe of sawgrass just off the beach, and a man with a gun could be hidden there waiting for me to make myself an easy target.

I sat down again, took the handkerchief from my face and checked the area with my fingers. The bleeding had stopped. I touched the little gouge mark on the boat where the first bullet had hit. Someone was actually trying to kill me. This wasn't merely a warning. The bullets had come too close. If I'd not taken evasive action, I might be dead right now.

That realization did nothing to lift my spirits, but the thought of Rog did. I wished I had him to talk to. Then I told myself once again I had to stop running to him every time something happened. The smart thing to do— and I didn't need anyone to tell me—would be to pack and go home. But I was angry as well as frightened. And frustrated. Granted that my research had worried the islanders, surely no one would resort to murder to stop my work!

I gunned the engine and held it at top speed all the way down to the channel until I turned to make port at the marina. There I eased the boat into the slip I'd been using, tied it up and walked briskly to the center of town.

I passed several people on my way, but I looked straight ahead. I didn't know if they'd speak or not, and I was in no mood to exchange idle pleasantries. I knew I should go directly to the mainland and enlist the aid of more competent authorities. I also knew they'd tell me to leave. Not that they wouldn't attempt to find whoever had fired at me, but whoever had done so wouldn't be fool enough to remain around, since he knew he hadn't killed me. Perhaps he wouldn't try again . . . perhaps he would. And the next time I might not be alive to worry about who it was!

And yet, I asked myself, what was I doing here? If I wished to report it to the proper authorities, I should go to the mainland. Or phone. I'd do the latter, and so I continued on to the hotel.

Mr. Tabor was at the desk conversing with a gentleman of about forty. He was dressed in light blue slacks and dark, double-breasted blazer. They fit his corpulent figure so well, they had to be tailor-made. His graying hair was combed straight back and rather long, but it was carefully barbered.

Mr. Tabor turned to me as I approached the desk. "Mornin', Miss Dexter. You look kinda mad."

"I am," I said bluntly. "I've just been shot at."

The stranger regarded me curiously. "Shot at?"

I touched my cheek. "A splinter of wood knocked off my boat by a bullet, did this. I heard the whine of a second shot, but thank heavens, that didn't come so close."

"Who'd want to shoot at you?" the stranger asked.

"If I knew that, I'd be on the phone calling the mainland and giving the name of the would-be assassin."

"Miss Dexter is the lady who leased the house you just bought," Mr. Tabor said.

The stranger nodded courteously. "How do you do, Miss Dexter. My name's Upton. Hal Upton. From Boston."

"I hope you don't want to take immediate possession," I exclaimed.

He regarded me incredulously. "You mean you intend to stay there after what just happened?"

"It happened on the water," I said.

He smiled at my statement. "You're a very brave young woman. I know the castle is isolated. I also think that if someone deliberately shot at you and missed, he might try again, hoping for better luck the next time."

"I'm going to see to it there won't be a next time," I said.

"How do you intend to accomplish that?" he asked.

"I'm not sure," I said. "But I'll be extra cautious. I

know I'm not popular on the island, but I didn't think anyone would go so far as to attempt murder to prevent me from carrying out my work."

Mr. Tabor had listened attentively, his expression smug. Now he said, "Miss Dexter hails from Salem. Or her ancestors did."

"What's that got to do with her being shot at?" Mr. Upton asked.

"A great deal, I'm afraid," I said.

Mr. Tabor said, "Mr. Upton, did you know the place you just bought is called Witch's Castle? First owner was a witch. Her name was Sarah Dexter. Lived there over a hundred years ago. This Miss Dexter hails from Salem."

"Pennsylvania," I said tersely.

"Your ancestors came from Salem," he said stubbornly. "Your papa even said you could be a descendant of hers."

"He was only joking," I replied. "Whether I am or not, I don't believe in witches."

Mr. Upton said, "Don't upset yourself, Miss Dexter. You've had enough for one morning."

I managed a smile. "Indeed, I have. However, I'm still hoping that you're not going to ask me to leave the castle."

"And I'm surprised you wish to remain there."

"I just decided I'm stubborn."

"With a touch of reckless bravado thrown in," Mr. Upton said, laughing. "No, Miss Dexter, I'll not put you out. I'm not interested in taking occupancy until the weather breaks late next spring."

"I'll be gone long before then," I said.

"You sure will, the natives got anything to say about it," Mr. Tabor said. His eyes flicked to Mr. Upton. "She's bent on keepin' our folks from makin' a livin'."

"That isn't true," I replied.

Mr. Upton looked interested. "What is your work, Miss Dexter?"

90

"I'm checking the channel for pollution."

"I approve of that," he said. "Will you join me at breakfast and tell me about it? That is, if you have an appetite after what happened to you."

"I believe I have," I said, smiling. "And thanks for asking me."

We were the only diners, for the hotel proper was closed. Mr. Upton told me he'd had to bribe Mr. Tabor yesterday to open a room for him, but he was fortunate in that the dining room wouldn't be closed for another week.

"I know," I said. "That's why I had to find quarters elsewhere."

The waitress who took our order was competent and, much to my surprise, friendly. Perhaps because of Mr. Upton. Though he was obviously a man of wealth, his manner was affable and he had a way of making a person feel at ease.

"I had no idea the house was about to be sold," I said.

"I was here some weeks ago and became quite enchanted with the place. Of course, I intend to do some extensive redecorating. I only came here last night to close the deal. As for you, Miss Dexter, you may remain there as long as you wish—if your work takes longer than your lease, you may live there, rent free."

"You're very kind. But I hope to have it completed before three months. I doubt I'd be rugged enough to spend the winter here."

"I know I wouldn't be," he chuckled. "Please tell me about your work. Have your discoveries so far been of an alarming nature?"

Before I could reply, our breakfast arrived, and it was a hearty one, consisting of grapefruit, ham, fried eggs and potatoes, hot rolls, jam and a large pot of coffee. It was all served at once, since the cook-waitress was the only employee. She told us she'd look in on us later and see if we wanted more, but we assured her what we had would do.

The grapefruit was sweet and juicy and after my first bite, I discovered I was famished. Mr. Upton noticed and smiled.

"I'm afraid I haven't paid much attention to food," I said.

"I'm glad I invited you."

"So am I," I said, returning the smile.

"But I'd still like to know just what it is you're looking for."

"I'm sorry to say what I've found isn't good. I've discovered traces of mercury in fish livers, and the plankton are seriously affected. The oyster and clam larvae are sparse too, because the food they need to survive was killed by poison."

"How bad is this mercury poisoning I've heard so much about?"

"Mr. Upton, if enough mercury compounds are ingested, they can cause early senility; they can maim and kill; they can produce brain damage in the unborn. The stuff has been indiscriminately dumped into the waterways and into the sea from a number of sources. The ocean was considered a safe place for disposal because it's so tremendous in size, but it's not that big near the shorelines, and that's where the metal salts seem to settle."

He whistled softly. "I heard that fishermen in some northern lakes were advised not to eat their catch. I thought it was just propaganda for some cause or other."

"It's extremely serious," I said. "Mercury compounds are used everywhere. Seed is treated with them so they won't be destroyed when they're put in the ground. That's one reason why we've had so many bumper crops. But rain washes the mercury away and it finally seeps down to the rivers. They empty into the seas and the poison is spread. It does great good at one end of the cycle and tremendous damage at the other."

"Strange how we don't realize what's happening until it's right on top of us. You may remain in that house as long as you please, even beyond the winter. My moving in is far less important than your work."

"I'm grateful, Mr. Upton. But I have to complete my work as soon as possible so I can get my thesis in. And I want to accumulate enough factual evidence to submit to the authorities so that this village can be warned, even prepared, in case all fishing is banned here."

"That would wreck the village," Upton said. "Go slow on that phase of it, please. I'd hate to come and live on a deserted island."

"It won't be too late to take proper action," I told him confidently. "If you'd like to come out to the castle to look around . . ."

"Oh no. I know what it looks like and I understand it's haunted. Have you witnessed any phenomena? It would make an interesting topic of conversation when I go back, telling my friends what's awaiting me here. They'll be on bended knees for an invitation to come up and see for themselves."

"As you know, the poor lady who is supposed to have been a witch was named Sarah Dexter. I think she was treated horribly by the villagers of that period."

"I conjure up a vision of someone very ugly."

"Oh no. She was an extremely beautiful woman. I saw her portrait."

He nodded in friendly fashion. "Then it's possible she could be an ancestor of yours. Is one of her cheeks dimpled?"

"If so, it wasn't evident in the portrait," I said blithely. I touched my napkin to my lips. "Thank you for a delightful breakfast, Mr. Upton. And please feel free at any time to come to the castle."

93

He arose and moved my chair for me. "I give you my word I'll not disturb you. I'm glad I met you and I wish you every success in your work."

"Thank you, Mr. Upton." Impulsively, I extended a hand. He grasped it lightly, then escorted me to the door. I was so pleasantly relaxed by his company and the excellent breakfast, I didn't even think to notice if Mr. Tabor was in evidence as I passed through the lobby.

I'd decided to shop for more groceries and was already on my way when Mr. Upton called to me. I turned around.

"You didn't call the police on the mainland, Miss Dexter."

I'd really forgotten about it, but I made a spur-of-the-moment decision. "I'm not going to. At least, not immediately. I want to finish my work and I'm afraid they'll insist I leave."

"They might, at that," he agreed and waved a farewell.

I waved back, noticing that Mr. Tabor was standing in the doorway. Obviously, he'd been watching for my departure and just as obviously he'd report to someone what he'd heard. I was beginning to think Mr. Tabor played a role of some sort in the conspiracy to get rid of me. Even if it was merely the role of observer, it was an important one, for he was in a position to get and pass on information which could increase the danger in which I'd placed myself.

I got my groceries and returned to my craft. I pulled away from the marina and opened up the engine for a quick run back. I still had my trap plates to examine.

ELEVEN

I reached the old pier without incident and I went directly to the castle, where I stowed away the supplies I'd bought. Then I went to work on the traps.

I removed the thin layer of scum, transferring it to a beaker. I filled this with sea water and then proceeded to place samples under the low power of my microscope.

I discovered the usual marine flagellates, the tiny sea worms, diatoms in profusion, but larvae so sparse it was hard to find. Now I accumlated the scrapings from every plate and used this to examine for mercury. My tests were necessarily simple because I lacked space and apparatus, but there was no question that the metal was present in formidable quantities. The chemical plant on the mainland was still pouring its pollutants into the sea. Before long, my test plates would capture nothing, and the shore waters would be barren of life.

By the time I'd finished this work, I was fuming over the gross carelessness of the factory owners. I was in a perfect mood to write letters to local newspapers, to the federal bureaus involved and to the governor.

The sound of an approaching automobile distracted me and brought me to the front porch. I watched a yellow Cadillac bounce over the ruts until it came to a stop directly before the castle. Its only occupant was a young woman. She got out of the car and strode briskly toward me. She looked stunning in deep pink slacks and sweater, topped by a purple cape. She was tall, slender and blonde, and her attractive oval features were softened in a smile of greeting.

I returned the smile and said, "Hello," as she ascended the stairs.

"Hello, Gale Dexter," she replied cheerfully. "I'm Libby Mayne. My dad owns the chemical plant on the mainland. Word has just come to him that you're checking the waters around here. He also heard you're both young and attractive. I agree."

I said, "Thank you, Miss Mayne."

"Make it Libby, please. Keep it friendly."

I laughed. "You've no idea how happy it makes me to hear you say that. When you identified yourself, I was afraid you'd come here to tell me you resented what I was doing."

"Quite the opposite," she assured me. "I'm here to assure you my dad wishes to cooperate in every way possible."

I sobered. "I'm grateful. Won't you come in, please?"

"I certainly will," she said. "I'd like to see this place that's supposedly haunted by a vengeful witch."

"That's not true," I said, leading the way inside.

"I know," she replied kindly. "But it makes a good topic of conversation for the natives—particularly with the summer visitors. They're very impressed. I imagine there are a million embellishments on the original story."

"Probably," I agreed. "Though I've not heard any."

She looked skeptical. "Really?"

I nodded. "The natives dislike me. I think I could use a stronger word in view of what happened a few hours ago."

"What do you mean?"

I touched my cheek. "I was shot at, while in my boat. The bullet missed me, but chipped off a piece of wood which struck me."

She stepped closed and studied my cheek. "So I see. I hope you called the state police?"

"I was going to, but then changed my mind."

"Don't you think that's being a little reckless?"

"Perhaps. But I'm working on my thesis for my Ph.D. and I'm afraid the police will insist I leave here if I report what happened."

She looked thoughtful. "They probably would. And yet it's so difficult to imagine any villager would resort to that."

"Not when you consider that my findings may deprive them from making a living."

"Good heavens, is it that serious?"

"I'm afraid it is."

"You know, it may be whoever shot at you, intended merely to frighten you away from here."

"I'm hoping that's it, though the bullet came too close for comfort. I heard the whine of a second bullet which, I'm thankful to say, didn't even hit the boat."

"Then I guess their idea is really to terrify you so you'll pack up and go."

"I've formed the same opinion." I told her about the pot of birds which I found stewing on the range last night.

"You have a lot of courage staying here."

"I don't know how much of it is courage and how much just plain stubbornness. May I offer you coffee?"

"Ordinarily, I'd say yes, but I just left Miss Mary and I had a very delicious lunch there."

"So you know her," I said.

She smiled. "I didn't until today. I was on my way here and she flagged me down with a lace handkerchief, started up a conversation, and before I knew it, I was telling her all about me and how I was on my way to visit you."

"It sounds like her."

"She told me you weren't home and insisted I come in. I did and, much to my surprise, her table, with lunch already on it, was set for two. It was as if she'd invited me beforehand and I'd arrived at the proper moment."

I contained my surprise. "She's a very gracious lady."

"But how did she know I was coming here?"

"She may have used binoculars and saw you and your car on the ferry heading for the island."

Libby's head moved wonderingly from side to side. "You may be right. I asked her, but she just gave me a mysterious sort of smile and said she just knew."

"Let's go in the living room and sit down," I said.

"Would you mind showing me through the house first? It looks quite interesting."

"It is," I said. "It even has a secret panel in my room which opens to reveal a stairway to the attic."

"Fascinating," she exclaimed. "I must see it."

I brought her to the second floor and she examined the rooms with great interest. She exclaimed over the sewing room with its dummies, old sewing machines and the dais on which one stood while getting a fitting. In my bedroom, the candelabrum which opened the panel leading to the attic stairway, delighted her, and she opened and closed it a couple of times.

She was fascinated by the dining room table, a

marvel of workmanship which she was sure dated back over a century ago. She thought my using part of the kitchen as a laboratory quite clever and pointed to various pieces of apparatus, inquiring as to how they worked and what their purpose was. We returned to the living room then and sat in the cushioned windowseat which gave us a clear view of the ocean.

"I mustn't forget my reason for coming," she said wryly.

"It concerns my work," I replied tolerantly.

"Yes," she said. "But having met you, I hope you'll let me return. I'd like us to be friends."

"Believe me, I could use one here," I said.

"Of course, I've done some reading on the ecology thing and I'm in firm agreement that things have gotten out of hand. However, my dad is hurt that you regard him as an ogre."

"But I don't," I protested.

"Oh, not him specifically. But he feels he's done a lot of good. He's run the plant for more than forty years. It manufactures insecticides, among other things. We both realize that dumping waste from such chemicals is dangerous to plant and animal life. Yet, in all fairness, even you must admit the insecticides have done much good. Crops have doubled and trebled. Seeds that were in the past destroyed after being in the ground for a few hours, now survive because they are treated with mercury. Fungus, mold and insects stay away from them and the farmer benefits."

"While river and sea life perish." I spoke without bitterness because there were two sides to this problem.

"True," she admitted. "The specific reason my dad sent me is that you were seen doing something or other near the outflow of our waste pipe. I suppose you were taking specimens of the water."

"I was. Will you please come back to the lab so I can show you exactly what I found?"

"Be glad to."

We returned to the kitchen. "I was seen retrieving plates which had been immersed in the water to collect ocean life. There was very little and in it was contained enough mercury compounds to create the precipitate in this test tube." I held up the tube for her to see. "Which means the water around that pipe is heavy with poison."

She nodded. "That's what dad was afraid of. He asked me to tell you the plant will begin burying the waste matter from now on."

I shook my head. "That won't do. Water will seep through the earth and get at it, wash it down to the sea. It takes such a small amount to do a great deal of damage."

"How then?" she asked in a puzzled voice.

"Change the compounds chemically into something inert. Don't ask me how. I'm no expert on that, and although I've studied chemistry, I'm not capable of setting up such a chemical transformation."

"Will you report it?"

"I'll feel obligated to unless it stops."

"It will stop," she assured me. "Just give us time to attend to the matter. My dad will go to work on it immediately."

"That's good news because, since I came here and began to test, I'd refuse to eat fish or mollusks taken from these waters."

She looked worried. "As bad as that? It makes me feel like an ogre."

"You shouldn't," I told her. "Nor should your dad— provided he takes immediate steps to stop polluting the waters."

"I must go now," she said. "Thanks for giving me so much of your time."

"Thanks for expressing an interest by coming here," I said. "You have no idea how grateful I am."

"I'm the one to be grateful," she said. "Because I'm the one the villagers should be pointing a finger at—not you."

"I can't convince them my motives are honorable," I said. "Did you know they believe I'm a descendant of Sarah Dexter?"

"Are you?" she asked curiously.

"I doubt it," I said smiling. "Though I don't know definitely."

Her brows lifted in sudden awareness. "So that's it. They think you've come here to get revenge for what their ancestors did to her. Or tried to do to her."

"I'm afraid that's it," I said.

"A lot of them are employed at dad's plant. Perhaps when they learn of my visit—and they will—they'll change their attitude toward you."

"It would make my life a lot more bearable here," I said.

"I'll work on it," she assured me with a smile. "May I come back?"

"Please do," I said.

"And when you're at the mainland, come visit me," she said. "I'm at the plant a great deal. I have an office there. I'll have to take over one day, so in the meantime I'm trying to learn every angle of the business."

"Thanks, Libby. I'll look forward to seeing you again —either here or on the mainland."

I accompanied her to the porch and waved a farewell as she headed back to the village and the ferry which would take her to the mainland.

TWELVE

It was sundown when Libby left. She would barely miss the tide. I lit two lamps, cleaned the laboratory, made some entries in my notebooks, read some more on the effect of mercury poisoning on ocean life and then decided to call it a day.

I hadn't caught even a glimpse of Roger, and I wondered what he did with himself all day—in fact, what he did at any time, for he'd never volunteered any information about his work.

It had been a long and somewhat tiring day, so I decided to retire early. The wind began to howl about the time I was putting out the lamps and locking up. It was worse by the time I got into bed. Not that these brief, but often sudden blows are rare here, but I wished they'd happen in the daytime when one's imagination was not stirred by moans and shrieks and the distant pounding of the waves, or the protesting creaks of the castle. At least tonight there was no rain, though the sky was as black as pitch.

I sighed in resignation, blew out the lamp by my bedside and settled down in bed. There was another lamp on the dresser, still lit, and I debated whether or not to leave it lit all night. I gave myself a mental shake, telling myself my fears were childish. If I was going to live here, I had to stop being frightened by sounds. I'd never been afraid to remain alone in a house before, and I wouldn't allow myself to be now. I'd blow out the flame of the lamp and settle down for a night's rest.

Before I could do so, the bed moved in a tilting motion. I sat up in alarm and discovered the entire castle seemed to be moving, just as it had last night. As I watched, the lamp on the dresser began to slowly slide toward the edge, as if it were being pushed. I had the same sensation as last night—that a pair of giant hands had a grip on the castle and was gently rocking it.

I admit my nerves were beginning to jangle again, but I refused to panic. The bed tilted to the other side and the lamp started to slide in the opposite direction, only this time it gained momentum. I bounded out of bed and rescued it, bringing it to the bedside table. The movement of the castle continued for an hour, along with the howling winds and the protesting creaks of the castle as the temperature dropped. It was accompanied by dismal moans and groans that sounded like mournful spirits doomed to eternal wandering.

Gradually, the moaning stopped and, at the same time, the storm abated until there was no further noise in the house. Even the surf had ceased its angry pounding. I released my hold on the lamp, blew out the flame and fell asleep in seconds.

The morning began with another surprise. I was making breakfast when I heard the *putt-putt* of an outboard motor. Curious, I stepped onto the back porch which commanded a view of the pier. A dory, equipped with an outboard, was just making the turn to head for the pier. There seemed to be but one person in it.

I walked down toward the pier to meet whoever it might be. On the way, I had another surprise. I'd not even noticed that two slim poles had been set up between Roger's cabin and my home. He must have done that work while I was in the village.

I switched my attention back to the man in the dory. He tied up, placed several tools out on the pier; among them a spade, a pickax, a hoe and rake along with, of all things, a lawn mower.

He was heavily built, with dark red hair and a crop of the same hued whiskers. Not a full-grown beard, but a growth of only a few days, making it appear as if he shaved only when the mood struck him. His deep-set eyes squinted as he regarded me.

"You Miss Dexter?"

"I am. May I ask who you are and what you're doing here?"

"Name's Sam Vernon. Hired by Mr. Upton to landscape." He surveyed the barren slope leading up to the house. "Place sure needs it."

"I saw Mr. Upton yesterday morning. Strange he didn't tell me you'd be coming here."

"Didn't hire me until yesterday afternoon," Mr. Vernon spoke as he gathered up his tools. He headed up the slope, apparently having ended the conversation.

But I'd not be so easily dismissed and took a few quick steps to catch up with him. "Do you live in the village, Mr. Vernon?"

"No'm. Mainland."

"Will there be any need for you to go in the castle?"

He turned to face me. "Would like a little hot water.

105

Certainly wouldn't go in to heat it without your permission. Favor it for tea."

"I'm not here always."

"Then I'll do without tea," he said, and resumed his walk to the house.

"No need for that," I replied. "I'll leave the back door unlocked. All I want to be assured of is that you'll not touch any laboratory equipment I've set up in the kitchen."

"You got my word, ma'am. Just want to boil some water. If you're fearful I'll make a mess, I'll do without."

"Indeed not," I replied. "Please feel free."

"Much obliged, ma'am. Promise I won't touch your food."

I smiled. "I don't have a very well-stocked pantry."

We'd reached the house and he set down his tools and looked around. Apparently, he was already eying the grounds, deciding on where to start first. It was a challenge to any landscaper's ingenuity, for the place was barren, with dead trees and sparsely growing weeds. And yet, there was something about this man that troubled me. I glanced at his hands, hoping it would give me a clue as to whether or not he was telling the truth. But it was almost impossible to tell, for there was a heavy growth of reddish hair on the back of his hands, continuing on down to his fingers. He walked away from me, his eyes still scanning the place.

On impulse, I headed for Rog's cottage, but I'd taken only a few steps when Mr. Vernon called my name.

"Just want you to know I won't go in the castle without you bein' there."

"The only reason I mentioned it, Mr. Vernon, is that some of my glass apparatus and chemicals are expensive and almost impossible to replace up here. Also, a few of the chemicals are very dangerous."

"No need to worry on my account. I won't touch 'em. Besides, I won't go in less'n you're there."

"Whatever you wish, Mr. Vernon."

I turned and continued on my way. Apparently, I'd hurt his feelings. I hadn't meant to, I'd spoken only what was on my mind—as he'd done. Just as I stepped onto Rog's porch, he opened the door, a smile of welcome widening his mouth.

"Hi, Gale. You're in time for breakfast."

"I'll settle for a cup of coffee."

"You'll have to share the omelette I made," he said.

"Don't tell me you're psychic like Miss Mary," I said. "You didn't really expect me, did you?"

"I heard the *putt-putt* of an outboard and saw you go down to the pier. If you hadn't headed this way, I'd have been out calling to you."

"Well, thanks. I was just preparing my breakfast when I heard my visitor."

Rog motioned me to the kitchen. "Who is he?"

"His name is Sam Vernon. He's from the mainland and told me Mr. Upton hired him yesterday afternoon to landscape the grounds."

"Mr. Upton?" Rog seated me, brought the pot from the stove and filled our mugs. The omelette was already on the table, along with a platter of crisp bacon. I cut a serving of omelette, placed several strips of bacon on the plate and handed it to Rog, then I served myself.

"He bought Witch's Castle and is moving in next spring."

"When did you learn that?"

"Yesterday morning in the village. I went there with fire in my eyes." I tasted the omelette. "It's delicious. You're an excellent cook."

"It's my hobby," he said, smiling. "Now that you've complimented me, please get on with your story."

"I was shot at yesterday when I was in my boat," I said.

He set his cup down abruptly. "Did you see anyone?"

"No. The bullet hit the boat. A bit of wood was chipped off and grazed my cheek."

He regarded the spot which was now scabbed over. "Why didn't you let me know?"

"I can't come running to you every time something happens," I said.

"You damn well can," he replied. "You have no one else to go to—other than the police. Is that why you went to the village?"

I nodded. "I went to the hotel to make the call, since I know of no public phones anywhere."

"There aren't any."

"When I went in, there was a stranger at the desk. Mr. Tabor introduced him as Mr. Hal Upton from Boston. He was very gracious and invited me to breakfast."

"What about notifying the police?"

"I changed my mind."

"That was smart." His tone and glance indicated he felt it quite the opposite.

"Perhaps not," I replied. "But I decided if I did, they might make me leave the island—for my own safety."

"I think that's a damn good idea," he replied. "Or do you like being shot at?"

"No," I retorted. "I don't like being lectured either."

His tone softened. "I'm not lecturing you. I'm concerned. Damn concerned. You're being foolish."

I smiled. "Mr. Upton said the same thing. But you know how important my work is to me. Whoever shot at me, missed. Probably he intended to. At least, that is the premise I'm going on. The discoveries I'm making in my work thus far, assure me I won't be here long."

"I'm of the same opinion, though not because of your work," he said dryly. "What else happened yesterday?"

"Something very nice. I met Libby Mayne. Do you know her?"

"I believe it was she I saw yesterday leaving Miss Mary's."

"Didn't you meet?"

"No. I was hiking across the field. She's an extremely attractive young woman."

"Extremely," I agreed, wondering if his interest was restricted to merely admiring her. "Anyway, her father owns the plant on the mainland which dumps waste into the ocean. The tests I made from water I took in that area are alarming. I showed her what I discovered."

"Is she concerned?"

"Both she and her father are, and she assured me he'd take immediate steps to correct the damage they're doing."

"How do they propose to go about it?"

"I don't know," I admitted. "That's their problem."

"Well, at least they're cooperating. More coffee?"

"Please." He filled both our cups. "I noticed the poles you put up yesterday."

"Sorry I didn't get the wires strung. I'll attend to it today."

"I'll appreciate it. I thought the castle was going to topple last night when that blow came up. The place actually seems to move. Even the lamp almost slid off the dresser."

"That's interesting," he commented. "Probably what frightened the last owners out of there. And several before them, no doubt."

I smiled. "Mr. Upton rather likes the story of the place being haunted. He believes his friends will be on their knees begging for an invitation once they hear the legend of Sarah Dexter."

"He's probably right," Rog said. "Particularly those who have nothing else to occupy their time. More coffee?"

"No thanks," I said.

He arose and carried the percolator back to the stove. He paused before a window and pulled the curtain aside.

"Your gardener is working, but somehow or other, it doesn't make much sense."

I arose and walked over to stand beside Rog. "What do you mean?"

"Winter's approaching. Who wants property landscaped now? You can't plant or transplant—even if he'd brought plants—which he didn't. Unless, of course, his intention is only to cut some of those old trees which are an eyesore. But landscaping at this time of year?"

"You know," I said, "that's really why I came here. I had that same opinion."

"I think Sam Vernon bears watching. I can do it easily since I'm going to string wires to the castle."

"Fine," I replied. "I'm going to the village and make a phone call to Mr. Upton and find out if he really sent Mr. Vernon. But let me do the dishes first so I can show my appreciation for the delicious breakfast."

"No," Rog said. "Get going. I can keep an eye on Vernon. I'll be outside stringing the wires."

There was no need to return to the castle, so I went directly to my boat, heading it into the channel in the direction of the village.

Mr. Tabor's eyes held a hint of surprise at sight of me. "Back again, Miss Dexter? What can I do for you?"

"I wish to make a phone call to Boston. It's urgent."

He eyed me contemptuously. "Emergency's about dyin' fish, I suppose."

"No, Mr. Tabor," I said firmly. "I wish to call Mr. Upton, concerning a man who came to the castle to landscape the premises. I wish to assure myself Mr. Upton really hired him. After all, I was shot at yesterday."

"That's different. Mind describin' him to me?"

I suppressed my impatience, knowing if I didn't, I might not get to make the call. "He says his name is Sam Vernon. He's a heavy-set, strong-looking man of about forty-five with dark red hair. Do you know him?"

Tabor shook his head. "You better call Mr. Upton. Can't take chances with a stranger."

"Thank you," I said.

I put through the call. A male voice in Mr. Upton's office answered and asked me to wait a moment. He came back on to say that Mr. Upton was away and there was no method by which he could be contacted. It seemed he was en route somewhere. I told the gentleman, who finally identified himself as Mr. Upton's secretary, about Sam Vernon and the story he'd given me, and said I wanted his employment by Mr. Upton verified. The secretary told me he'd speak to Mr. Upton about it the first time he called in. I thanked him and gave the phone number of the inn.

"Mr. Upton's away," I told Mr. Tabor. "You heard what I said. He'll likely call you and I'll appreciate it if you'll let me know if Mr. Vernon's all he claims to be."

Mr. Tabor assured me he'd send word if Vernon was lying, then asked, "How soon you leavin' Witch's Castle?"

"I'll probably be there at least two months or longer."

"I mean how soon before you'll be scared out of there like everybody else was?"

"I'll leave when my work is completed, not one hour before."

"Lady, if you stay there, it's 'cause you're one of 'em, and 'cause you are, they don't make things move about or start hollerin' in the night."

"Mr. Tabor, if I were a witch, I might be in a position to know who shot at me. Also, I might know if Mr. Vernon was all he says he is."

"How'd you go about doin' that?" he asked belligerently.

"I'd cook up a stew of dead birds and look into the pot and the truth would be revealed."

His face flamed—if not with guilt, then with an awareness of the foul-smelling stew which had been placed on

111

my range. It made me more certain than ever that a group of islanders were behind the attempt to frighten me away from here. I turned then and headed for the door. On my way out, I noticed two men seated before the windows which looked out onto the street. Neither glanced my way and I thought no more about it.

Latest U.S. Government tests of all cigarettes show True is lower in both tar and nicotine than 99% of all other cigarettes sold.

Think about it.
Shouldn't your next cigarette be True?

Regular and Menthol: 12 mg. "tar," 0.7 mg. nicotine, av. per cigarette, FTC Report Apr. '72.

Latest U.S. Government
tests of all menthol
cigarettes show
True is lower
in both tar and
nicotine than 99% of
all other menthols sold.

Think about it.
Shouldn't your next cigarette be True?

©Lorillard 1972

THIRTEEN

On my way back, I sailed out to my traps and re-covered them, putting new ones in their place. Then I spent three hours cruising about, getting samples with my ZoBell bottles at three different depths in five locations. I now had sufficient laboratory work to keep me occupied the rest of the day, so I headed back.

Mr. Vernon was still at work, if one could call leaning on a hoe work. He got busy as I pulled in, but he didn't pause to greet me as I passed, hoeing energetically on some hard-packed, barren earth. I felt a vague uneasiness regarding him and I wondered if he'd been inside the castle.

Nearing it, I saw the wires strung from the poles and spliced in with the old wires at the meter box attached to the side of the castle. I now had electricity and it was most heartening.

In the castle, I checked my apparatus and chemicals carefully. Nothing had been disturbed, so I tied on my lab apron and provided myself with the few sterile slides I had left. From now on, with the use of electricity, I could put my little autoclave to work and have all the sterile slides I wished.

I obtained the same results as last time. Very few larvae, which meant depopulated, barren oyster beds, few clams, fewer lobsters and crab. The village was going to have a most unsuccessful season when it came time to harvest the sea once again.

Some of the slides were too good to discard, so I made a permanent sample of the work I was doing. If anyone wanted instant proof, I had it now. The plankton and larvae I'd trapped were the smallest, sickliest specimens I'd seen in all of my brief career.

With the artificial light in my microscope, I could work faster and with more accuracy. At dusk, when I snapped a switch and the kitchen glowed with bright light, I felt as if I'd been reborn. I wished Roger would stop in, so I could thank him for his efforts.

It proved to be a pleasant and warm evening. I had no more pressing work to do, so I left Witch's Castle to walk about the island tip and enjoy the sea air and the moonlight.

I wandered down to the pier and was startled to see Sam Vernon's outboard still tied up. I thought that strange. He'd made no mention of remaining here overnight. Certainly there was nowhere for him to stay, unless he was in the castle without my knowledge. I'd check to see, for that I'd not countenance.

I heard a motor of some kind and I peered out to sea, but the moonlight wasn't bright enough for me to make out the shape of any sort of boat. Then I realized the sound came from behind me. Presently, a single headlight penetrated the darkness and I knew it was Roger, riding his motorcycle. He must have gone to the village.

I walked briskly to his cottage. He was getting off his motorbike as I approached, and he used a flashlight to identify me, though being careful not to shine it directly into my face. He slipped an attaché case from one of the handlebars, tucked it under his arm and turned his attention to me.

"Hi, Gale. Has something else happened?"

Despite my concern, I had to smile. "I don't wonder you ask. It seems each time I come here, something has."

"Just so long as you come. What is it?"

"Mr. Vernon's boat is still tied up at the pier. He's nowhere about. Do you know if someone came for him?"

"I didn't see anyone, but I've been to the village. Twice, in fact. I had to go to the mainland today for wire. I didn't have nearly enough."

My spirits dropped. "Then you weren't in a position to watch him."

"Sorry I let you down," he said. "Did you check the castle to see if he might have appropriated a room there?"

"No. I thought I'd check with you first."

"You're hurt," he said.

"A little," I admitted. "Somehow or other, I don't trust him. I was unable to contact Mr. Upton, but his secretary will check with him the first time he calls in. Either he hasn't returned or he's off somewhere."

"So Vernon's boat is still at the pier."

"Yes. I wonder if he walked to the village."

"Hardly—when he has a boat. And that man's lazy. When he wasn't leaning on his shovel, he was sitting on the back porch smoking a pipe. I'll check my cottage, then we'll make a thorough search of the castle. Want to come in?"

"No. I'll wait here."

He made no reference to the attaché case, but then,

there was no reason why he should, However, the sight of it did pique my curiosity, particularly since when he came out, he still carried it under his arm. However, I was too concerned with Vernon's absence to give it more than a passing thought.

We made a thorough search of the castle without finding any trace of the man. We walked further inland, returned to scout the very tip of the island. The outboard floated peacefully at the end of the pier, but there was no sign of Vernon.

"Let's try the castle again," Roger suggested. "We skipped the cellar."

The chances of his having gone down the stairs to the cellar were extremely remote because they were festooned with cobwebs that Roger had to brush away with a broom we had found in the pantry. Using the flashlight, we searched in corners and behind barrels without finding any trace of him. I was attracted to a plank-covered area of the cellar and I called Roger's attention to it.

"That would be a well," he said. "They used to dig them and then build the house over them." He pried up one of the heavy pieces of lumber, then asked me to pick up a large chunk of old masonry, lying on the basement floor, and drop it down the shaft. It landed some seconds later, not with a splash, but a faint thud.

"It's dry," Roger said, replacing the plank. "Your water comes from an outside well and my cottage shares it. I think I'd better take these planks off. The ray of my flash will reach down there."

"Oh no," I cried out.

"Don't get alarmed needlessly. The chances are practically nil that he's down there because those pieces of lumber haven't been moved in a long time. But we'll just make certain."

He lifted away more of the covering lumber and then shot the beam of his flashlight down the shaft. It showed rough stone walls and a dry base. There was no mangled corpse at the bottom of it. Roger covered it again and we went upstairs.

"I don't know where he is," Roger said. "The only answer is that he walked to the village. We don't know when he left, so he might have made the proper tide. Nothing more we can do. We checked the whole tip of the island and we know he can't be here. Let's check his boat. I'm sure it's empty, but I'd rather be doubly sure."

We left the house through the kitchen. We'd almost reached the pier when Rog used his flash to survey the area where Vernon's boat was tied up. But there wasn't a sign of it. He uttered an exclamation of surprise, walked swiftly ahead and used his flash for a hasty inspection of the dock. When I joined him, he pointed to the pier. The side of it, where Vernon would have stepped into his boat, was soaked with seawater while the rest of the pier was perfectly dry.

"But how did he get away without making enough noise to alert us?" I asked.

"He rowed. Far enough out so we wouldn't hear the sound of the outboard when he started it. What I want to know is, why all this water on the pier?"

"And where in the world was he when we were searching?" I asked.

"He wasn't in the castle and he wasn't in my cottage, that's for sure. Other than those two places, there's nowhere he could have been hiding. No brush, no forest, no barn, not even a shed. And yet, he was here somewhere."

I borrowed Roger's flashlight and threw the beam over the pier all the way to land. "There's plenty of water where we're standing, but he didn't come across the pier soaking wet, because the rest of it is bone dry."

"That's right. The only explanation I have, he was in the water."

117

"All that time?" I queried.

"Tomorrow," Roger said, "Mr. Sam Vernon is going to do some explaining—if he returns. At any rate, he's gone."

Roger escorted me back to the castle, but neither of us had much to say. I knew he was as puzzled about Sam Vernon as I. However, I was also puzzled about Roger Randall and that attaché case. He held it under his arm all the time we were together—even when he was lifting those heavy planks. I wondered what it contained. I also wondered just why Roger Randall was staying here.

I thought too of Miss Mary. Was she as innocent and naïve as she pretended? Was she gifted with second sight? Did she know something about the castle no one else did? Or was it just that she liked to play-act? These questions and more plagued me long after I retired.

Also, for the first time, I felt a deep loneliness. I didn't have to wonder why. I knew. Though I'd wanted no romantic entanglements, I was beginning to think of Rog Randall as more than a friend in need. But after the rebuff I'd given him when he kissed me, he'd made no further attempt to treat me as other than a friend. I should have been grateful. I told myself I was, for I was indebted to him. I was imposing on his friendship by enlisting his aid each time an emergency or problem arose. But could I stop? I had no one else to turn to. No one on the island treated me as a human being except Miss Mary. And while I knew she wasn't fey, she did seem to be playing a little game with me. But then, why not? She was lonely, and certainly, though I'd known her only briefly, I couldn't help but feel a fondness for her.

FOURTEEN

The mood of the season was displayed in next morning's weather. It was bleak, gray and chilly. The sea was calm enough, but I wore a heavy pea jacket when I set out to collect more samples. I saw smoke curling from the chimney of Roger's cottage. His motorbike, parked in front, gave evidence of his presence.

As I prepared to move away from the pier, I heard Sam Vernon's outboard coming in. I waited until he pulled up alongside me. He waved a hand in greeting, but made no attempt to converse.

"Mr. Vernon," I said, "when did you leave last evening?"

"When? What do you mean, ma'am?"

He knew very well what I meant. "Your boat was still here after ten o'clock."

"Yes'm, I know. I headed back about ten-thirty, I guess."

"And where did you spend the time between dusk and that hour? You weren't at work."

"No'm. Anything but that. Worked hard all day and got real tuckered, so I just crawled under the pier on the warm sand and went to sleep. But I did a full day's work, ma'am. Nobody can say I didn't."

I knew he was referring to Roger, who had promised to keep an eye on Sam Vernon. "I'm not questioning the work you do. But if you plan to nap here again, let me know so I won't worry about you."

He chuckled. "No one worries about Sam Vernon. He can take care of himself."

I believed it. "I'm going out to collect some specimens. I'll be back in two or three hours."

"I'll be here, ma'am. I'll be here."

I'd have been much happier if he'd said he'd not be. The rest of the day was uneventful enough. Vernon pretended to work, Roger remained secluded in his cottage. At least, I thought that's where he must be, for the motorbike was still parked outside. I did notice him twice that afternoon. I'd gone to the second floor to rest for a while and from one of the bedroom windows, I'd seen him standing outside his cottage where he had a good command of the sea, peering through a telescope. Apparently, binoculars weren't sufficient for his spying. He had to do it with a more powerful instrument. More and more, I was wondering about his presence on the island. I liked him enormously, but he never offered any information about himself, though he was not in the least recluctant about asking me questions.

Late in the afternoon, the Cadillac roared up. My spirits lifted when I saw Libby Mayne striding toward the castle, engulfed in a huge fake fur coat.

"I'm the bearer of a message," she said, "from Mr.

120

Tabor, though his wife relayed it to me. A Mr. Upton phoned him and said he had not hired anyone to do any work around this house. I don't know what it means, but that's what I was told to tell you."

"Mr. Upton just purchased this property. Mr. Tabor was referring to a man named Sam Vernon, who showed up yesterday and said Mr. Upton hired him to landscape it."

"Landscape Witch's Castle?" She looked amused. "And at this time of year?"

"That's what made me suspicious, so I went into town and tried to contact Mr. Upton."

"I heard all about it. Mrs. Tabor is very angry with you."

"Now what have I done?"

"Put a hex on Mr. Tabor. She told me her husband said you threatened to do it the last time you were there."

"I did no such thing."

Libby laughed. "What's your secret, girl? I could use a little of that black magic myself on a few people I know."

"Please, Libby. This isn't funny."

She sobered. "I know it isn't. And I wish I could help. I tried to persuade Mrs. Tabor you were as normal as I, but I was merely wasting words."

"What's it all about?"

"Mr. Tabor is very ill. His doctor can't diagnose his illness. He's gone through every test he could do outside of a hospital, to which Tabor refuses to go. Tabor claims it's your work—black magic. What happened the last time you were there?"

I sighed. "Mr. Tabor made me angry. He said that if I stayed at Witch's Castle, it was because I was a witch and those of my kind wouldn't frighten me the way they'd frightened other owners. I told him if I were a witch, I'd cook some dead birds, look in the broth and see who shot

121

at me. From his reaction, I gathered he knew all about the kettle of vile broth I found on my stove."

"I'd forgotten about that."

I told her briefly all that had happened since I arrived here.

"How horrible," she said. "I'll tell my dad about it and see if he can't talk sense to the villagers who work at his plant. He already has men working on ways of disposing the waste."

"I'm pleased to hear it, Libby. After having met you, I'd hate to have to submit a report."

"I'm grateful you won't," she said. "I just wish the villagers could get it out of their heads you're the descendant of Sarah Dexter."

"If not *the* Sarah Dexter," I said with a smile.

She nodded. "There are even those who think that, since witches don't die."

"How did you happen to see Mrs. Tabor?"

"I stopped at the inn for a cup of coffee. I wish I hadn't, except that you should be warned about this Sam Vernon, whoever he is. What are you going to do about him?"

"I have a friend at the cottage nearby, who can deal with Mr. Vernon better than I."

"Would your friend happen to ride a motorbike, have auburn hair, wear a heavy turtleneck sweater almost as blue as his eyes?"

I smiled. "It sounds like him."

"He's gorgeous, but he's not handy at the moment. He passed me, heading for the village."

I hadn't heard him leave. His bike made enough racket to waken a sound sleeper, but it hadn't reached me, even wide awake. He must have pushed it away until the distance to the castle prevented it from being heard. I wondered why he'd do such a thing.

"Anyway," Libby went on, "I came out to tell you, dad and I had a long conference with our laboratory people and they're going to try to eliminate the outflow of waste completely. It may take a little time . . . two or three weeks, they estimate, but it will be done."

"Libby," I said, "if all manufacturers in this country cooperated that well, we'd put an end to this water pollution problem. I'd like to do something in return, and I have an idea. I'll keep testing, making my entries, until the water clears. Then I'll have open-and-shut facts about what happens when the pollution stops because a factory owner thought more of the ecology than of profit. It will be a perfect example and I'll get it maximum publicity."

"Great," she said. "I didn't expect that, but it's welcome. Dad will be pleased."

"No more than I, Libby." I accompanied her to her car. She glanced in the direction of Sam Vernon. He was using a spade this time, like a man digging for worms before spending a lazy day fishing.

"I see what you mean," Libby said. "He's a rough-looking character. Don't go near him without your Roger by your side."

"He's not my Roger."

"From the way you look when you speak his name, I gather you'd like him to be." She glanced at Sam Vernon. "Wouldn't you like me to stay with you until your friend returns?"

"No need," I said. "Thanks again for driving out."

"Another bit of advice. Don't go into the village until they find out that Tabor has a perfectly simple disease and not just feeling poorly because he's been bewitched. The man's obsessed, but those people are eager to believe in anything concerning witchcraft, because they've lived with the history of it so long."

"I'll keep away," I promised. "Come back soon, Libby."

She nodded and drove off, leaving me with the feeling that I was very much alone. The sight of Vernon, prodding the spade into the ground and turning over about two inches of it, wasn't helpful. I went into the house and locked the door, front and back. That didn't reassure me too much, but I felt a little better.

I began to work, but stopped from time to time to see if Vernon was about. He kept in sight, playing at gardening. I spent the rest of the day in my lab and listened for the sound of Rog's noisy motorbike, indicating his return.

I spent an hour typing my findings and then, feeling lonely and restless, I went outside. Much to my surprise, Sam Vernon was nowhere about, but his outboard was still tied up. I wondered where he could be. This tip of the island offered limited places where a man could conceal himself. I didn't begin a search for him. In fact, I was pleased that I didn't have to encounter him, because the thought of him now made me uneasy.

Roger's motorbike was not in front of his cottage, so he hadn't yet returned. I got aboard my motorboat, started it and headed out to the channel. It was a bit too soon to harvest my plankton traps, but, to keep busy, I decided to have a look at them anyway. If there was sufficient film showing, I'd harvest them. Otherwise, it was a simple matter to put them back into the sea.

Five minutes after I left the pier, the engine sputtered ominously. I cut the speed and decided that I'd best go straight back. Repairing engines was not among my talents, and I didn't want to be caught adrift.

Before I completed half the turn, the engine died. It expired in such a way as to make me suspect I was out of gas, but I'd refueled at the village marina and used very little since then. The tank should have been three-fourths full.

I measured the contents and found the tank bone dry. It was no simple leak or I'd have smelled the gas. This meant the gas had been removed, and the sole purpose would have been to immobilize me well off shore.

I could swim back. I wasn't too worried about that, but the idea that someone had *wanted* me to be stranded out here was certainly not one to cheer me.

I could do for a while in the hope that when Rog returned, he'd see me. I was within easy sight of land. But he might not return for hours. I didn't even know where he'd gone, beyond the fact that Libby told me he was headed for the village. The alternative was to swim. I was not exactly in the mood for it. If I'd been wearing a bathing suit, it would have been different, but I was fully dressed. I'd have to shed most of my clothes to make the swim easier. I decided to wait a while, hoping Rog would come back, find me missing from the castle and my boat gone. If so, he would institute an immediate search for me, scanning the ocean first. I was clearly visible from land. Of course, all this was merely wishful thinking on my part; I even thought I might drift closer to shore.

A glance at my watch told me I had still a full hour to darkness, but after twenty minutes went by, I began to grow more nervous. The boat was moving further out, not swiftly, but quite surely. I decided to swim for it. I was about to remove some of my clothes, when I felt the boat give a violent lurch to port. I looked around. A man's hand was grasping the side of my boat. The back of the hand and the arm was covered with a heavy growth of reddish-brown hair. The second hand emerged from the water, holding a knife. While I watched in fresh terror, the end of a snorkel appeared, followed by the head and shoulders of the diver. There was no doubt who this was. Only Sam Vernon had this dark red hair and beard. The mask covered his face well.

He was trying to hoist himself aboard. I looked for some weapon to defend myself with, but there was nothing. I hastily removed one shoe and smashed the heel of it down on one of his hands. It must have hurt, because he dropped back into the water, but not for long. He came up, grasped the side of the boat again and started to rock it. The movement threw me off balance and I fell forward, almost going overboard. I was only inches away from him. His hand, holding the knife, thrust downward. I screamed and managed to push myself away just as the knife plunged into the seat where I'd fallen. Now I knew for certain he meant to kill me.

He used both hands now to hoist himself up and into the boat. I couldn't get near the knife. Even if I had been able to, I doubted I could have pulled it free of the seat. There was just one thing I could do: Go overboard and attempt to save myself by swimming. I was good, but I knew he was better. Yet, it was my only chance for survival.

Vernon was pulling himself up now. In a moment he'd be over the rail. I kicked off my other shoe and was about to slip over the side when I heard a whining sound and a sharp splash into the sea. I'd heard the sound before. Someone was shooting at us.

Vernon let go, dived, came up again a dozen yards away. The tiny water spout indicated another bullet must have struck close to him. He vanished. I managed to stand erect and look toward shore. Vernon's outboard was already leaving the pier. Guiding it was Rog Randall. He must have fired the shots to scare Vernon away. I lowered myself weakly to the padded seat near the wheel. One of my shoes was close by. I automatically put it on. I couldn't see the other one for the moment.

The outboard was moving fast. Now and then, Rog stood erect to scan the sea. I noticed he held a rifle. I didn't think Sam Vernon was swimming around the vicinity, though I did look for the tell-tale trail of his snorkel, without seeing it.

The outboard bumped against my boat. Rog threw me a rope and I tied it to the rail.

126

"I'm out of gas," I told him. "Vernon must have emptied my tank."

"So that's who it was," Roger said.

"Yes. He had a knife and he was going to kill me."

"Well, now we know what his purpose was, and you can report it to the State police. I'm coming aboard and rig the rope for towing. You can explain everything after we reach shore."

The outboard tow was not a speedy one, but as we moved steadily toward the pier, I lost the panic which had consumed me by the sudden appearance of a would-be murderer coming out of the sea.

When the two craft were secured to the dock, I thanked him for rescuing me.

His reply was simple. "I love you, Gale. I shouldn't have left you here with Vernon, but I did. Thank God, I came back in time."

I managed a smile. "I'm so indebted to you."

"Never mind that." He spoke almost gruffly. "Tell me what happened. Begin with the visit of Libby Mayne. I passed her on my way to the village."

"She came to tell me her father has his scientists working on eliminating polluting wastes from their factory. First, she stopped off at the hotel and Mrs. Tabor gave her a message from Mr. Upton for me. He did not hire Sam Vernon to landscape here."

Rog nodded. "We know that now."

"But why should he want to kill me?"

"I don't know. What else did she tell you?"

"That Mr. Tabor is ill and the doctor can't diagnose it without Tabor going to the hospital. He won't go."

"What's that got to do with you?"

"Everything. He believes now I'm a witch because I won't move out of the castle. He says I must be one of them; otherwise, I'd have been frightened out of here like the others were. Also, he claims I made him ill."

Rog smiled. "He excels at character assassination. You probably don't know it, but he and his wife have been largely responsible for the reincarnation of Sarah Dexter, witch. While the stories were still told, it was largely to give the island flavor and excite the interest of the tourists. But with your coming, the legend of Sarah Dexter was revived. It was easy to do because of your name."

"But why should the Tabors wish to do that?"

"That's what I'm trying to find out," Rog replied quietly. "I checked thoroughly today and learned that they're the ones who passed the word around you're Sarah Dexter's descendant."

"But Mr. Tabor is really ill, isn't he?"

"Is he?" Rog countered with a smile. "If a doctor can't make a diagnosis, there's obviously nothing wrong with the man."

"Did you talk with the doctor?" I asked.

"Yes."

"Does he think Tabor's faking?"

"He didn't come out and say so. He couldn't really. He merely stated Tabor's symptoms were vague, adding that probably he was tired after the busy season."

"I'm glad to hear it," I said, relief evident in my voice.

Rog looked amused. "You didn't really think you'd put a hex on him, did you?"

"I wish I could laugh at the idea," I said wearily. "But all that's happened has upset me too much. I've been shot at . . ." I paused suddenly and looked up at Rog. "That wasn't you, was it?"

"I swear it wasn't," he said. "I used Vernon's rifle to shoot at him, so I imagine it was he who shot at you, though I don't know. What we've got to do is find him and I think we'd better start now. I don't know if he'd return to get his boat or not. But I'll take his rifle out of it, just in case."

"Rog," I said, "I missed you today."

He'd started to turn, but paused, giving me a side glance. "Thanks. I thought you were aware of me only when you got frightened."

"I found out today I'm very aware of you. You kept intruding in my work, making concentration a little difficult. I was restless and lonely. That's why I went outside really—to see if you'd returned."

"What are you saying? Or is my imagination running away with me?"

"I . . . think that I love you, Roger. I'm afraid I resented you at first, perhaps because I found you too appealing and I felt my prime interest was my work. I came up here very dedicated."

"You still are," he said. "And don't apologize for it."

"Thanks," I said.

He took me in his arms then and kissed me. There was warmth in it and we were reassured by it, but there was no further love-making. We were still too aware of what Sam Vernon had tried to do.

Rog released me and got the rifle. "Let's check the castle first. He could have returned and hidden there, though I doubt it. He needs a more secure hiding place. The police will be searching for him, once we report his attempt to murder you."

On the way, I said, "You are here for a specific reason, aren't you?"

"Yes," came his firm reply. "But I can't talk about it."

"Why not? You said you love me. Love is trust, isn't it?"

"Definitely. And that applies to you also."

"But why can't you even give me a hint?"

"Because you're in enough danger now. I don't want it heightened by revealing my purpose for being here."

"What about Vernon?" I countered. "Do you know who he really is?"

"No. There are evil forces at work here. I said evil—not ghostly. And they don't concern Sarah Dexter—or you, even if you are her descendant. Now please don't ask me more. The less you know, the safer you'll be."

"I'm more confused than ever," I said. "As for being safer, I can't accept that. I couldn't possibly have been in greater danger since I came here."

"I'm sorry, Gale," he replied. "You'll just have to trust me."

"All right," I said. "But can you tell me this much—are you connected in any way with the work I'm doing here?"

"No."

"Then it's something more serious."

He nodded. "I believe Tabor's connected with it in some way. He's goaded the natives into a high form of resentment toward you. Now let's get on with our search."

And with that, I had to be content.

FIFTEEN

We made a careful inspection of the castle, then went outside to make a tour of the island tip. But we were unable to find a trace of Sam Vernon. On the way back to the castle, I regarded the burned skeleton of my car.

"Do you believe Tabor was responsible for that?" I asked.

"It was the first attempt to keep you from moving into the castle. Not many people knew you intended to, but he did."

"So did Mr. Abrams, the rental agent. Anyway, now that I have electricity—thanks to you—to dispel the gloom, will you have dinner with me?"

"Be glad to. I wouldn't leave you alone here anyway."

We reentered the castle through the kitchen door. I donned my laboratory apron after moving through the downstairs rooms flicking on light switches. It was so

131

exciting to have the place flooded with light, I was tempted to run outside and see its welcoming glow.

"I'm afraid dinner won't be much, since it will have to come mostly out of cans. But I *can* cook," I added earnestly.

His laugh was hearty. "Is that a new form of proposal?"

"I wouldn't be so presumptuous," I said, my glance teasing.

His arms scooped me up and this time, when our lips met, the flame of love fully enveloped us. I wondered how I hadn't fallen into his arms the first time our eyes met, for I felt weak with rapture. Yet, a spark of reason still remained and I slipped free of his embrace, but he caught me to him again, demanding one more kiss. With a happy sigh, I raised my face, reveling in his closeness, his dearness and his love.

When he released me, I went into the pantry and pressed my face against the coolness of the wall. I felt so happy I wanted to cry. Once I got hold of myself, I took some cans off the shelf for our dinner. From now on, I'd have a refrigerator and no longer be restricted in what I could buy.

We had dinner in the kitchen, but I did light a candelabrum to set a romantic mood. It wasn't difficult to keep our conversation light, for we had much to learn about each other. Afterward, he insisted on helping me with the dishes. The chore we performed didn't matter—it was doing it together and being together that made the moments precious. Before I removed my apron, I went to my laboratory bench.

"Excuse me one moment," I said. "I've got a culture going in that jelly glass."

He picked up the glass and held it to the light. "What's in here?"

"A little friend of mine named *ceratium.* In fact, a

132

few thousand friends of mine named *ceratium*. They're a marine dinoflagellate and they abound in the plankton. They're a great source of food for marine life. They're easy to count, and by their numbers you can get a good idea if the water has been poisoned or not. Want to see one?"

"Certainly."

I placed a drop of the water into a slide, added a cover glass, placed it on the microscope stage and turned on the light. I peered through the binocular lenses and gave a startled exclamation.

"What is it?" he asked.

"These critters move very fast, but this batch is just floating around."

"The water must be well poisoned."

"No. This water didn't come from the ocean. It was sea water I manufactured. That's why I had this colony growing, to see how fast they multiplied after they'd been exposed to pollution and managed to survive."

"I'm out of my element," he confessed.

I switched to a higher power. "They're not dead. I see signs of life, but they don't move. They act as if they're asleep."

"Maybe they were tired."

I gave him an annoyed look, the kind a scientist uses on the uninitiated who don't understand the importance of their work.

"This has to be accounted for. Let me think. I didn't use a sterile container to grow them in, because it wasn't necessary. There could have been something on the glass . . . but I rinsed it very carefully. The spoon . . . no, it was a spatula."

I rummaged in the kitchen drawer and found the green-handled dime-store spatula.

"I used this to add food for them. I didn't wash it . . ."

I went to work, pleased at his growing interest as I explained to him what I was doing.

"I have sea water containing these creatures, and a great number of others that I took from the ocean yesterday. The containers holding them were sterile, so there'll be no contamination there."

I sucked up a quantity of the sea water in a large pipette and transferred it to a beaker full of my artificial sea water. Then I dipped the spatula in the water.

"Whatever put them to sleep," I said, "was either in the jelly glass or on this spatula, so we'll try the spatula first."

I transferred some of the water to a slide and examined it. The microscopic creatures were moving, but not as fast as usual. Then, while I watched, they ceased to move altogether, but they remained alive. Other plankton acted in a similar manner.

"Whatever it is, was on the spatula," I said. "Not in the food I gave them."

He examined the spatula. "It looks clean to me."

"Most microscopic life," I said, "is highly susceptible to drugs. The spatula could look clean, but if there was a trace of some substance—the merest trace—it would affect them."

He pulled open the kitchen drawer from which I'd taken the spatula.

"The drawer is lined with paper," he observed. He began carefully lifting out each utensil, placing them to one side. He grasped the paper drawer lining in such a way as to capture any debris spilled on it.

"Got a hand lens?" he asked.

I supplied him with one, still puzzled as to what he was after. He studied the specks of debris on the paper. "Could you add this to another solution of bugs and see if it puts them to sleep too?"

"Of course." I prepared another culture from the sterile

container. I examined a drop of water under high power before adding the debris. There was lively plankton swimming about, dominated in numbers by the *ceratium*. I creased the drawer paper, let the specks drop into the culture, and transferred a drop to another slide.

"They're dead," I said, without removing my eyes from the twin lenses. "There was much more than a trace on that paper."

"Of what? Have you any idea?"

"Almost any type of narcotic."

"Heroin? Morphine?"

"Yes. As I said, any narcotic. A trace, an amount you couldn't possibly see, or perhaps even detect by chemical analysis, would put them to sleep. Any added amount would kill them."

He regarded the slide. "And these are dead?"

"See for yourself," I invited.

He peered through the lenses. "Dead all right. See if you agree with this theory. Someone brought a quantity of a narcotic into this kitchen. Maybe it was pure stuff and they were cutting it . . . diluting it. They'd use a tool like this spatula to lift the powder, transfer it to a scale, or to the dilutant. They might wipe the spatula afterwards and think it perfectly clean, but, from time to time, traces of narcotic fell into the drawer until there was enough to kill off those bugs in seconds."

I sat down heavily. "What are you saying?"

"That this house was being used as some kind of a cutting plant for illicit drugs."

"So that's why they're trying to frighten me away."

"This could be some kind of a relay station in a chain of drug smugglers."

"But who . . . ?" I began.

"That's the one thing it doesn't explain."

"Sam Vernon?" I suggested.

"No doubt he has something to do with it, but he's new

135

on the island. Nobody ever heard of him before. Chances are good nobody would have seen him—until you came along."

"It still can't account for everything that's happened. I agree my presence in this house may have been embarrassing for people who used it to prepare illegal drugs; yet, how do you account for the shaking of the house, the objects that moved, the groans and moans, and the voice calling to Satan."

"I can't, and I admit it doesn't sound like something a gang of drug smugglers would do, even if they were capable of it. From now on, I'm going to sleep in the sitting room, with a gun beside me. You're not safe here alone."

I smiled my gratitude. "It will be a big help. I do want to finish my work."

"Right now, I think we'd best go down to the pier and fill your boat with gas, just in case we need it in a hurry. Better get a coat."

I donned my pea jacket and joined Rog in the reception hall. We went out into the night.

He used his flashlight and we moved along at a fast gait because the night air was cold. We made our way along the pier, our heels thudding loudly in the silence. At the end of it, he placed me in charge of the rifle while he searched for tins in which he could carry fuel from his cottage.

Armed with three cans, we filled them from a supply he kept on hand for his motorbike. Back again at the pier, he clambered aboard my boat and began filling the tank. I heard him give a sudden, sharp cry.

"What is it?" I asked. I could see little in the dark.

"Just a minute," he said. "It may be nothing, but if it's what it looks like . . ."

He leaned far over the rail, throwing the beam of his flashlight onto the water. He straightened up and took off his coat and shirt. "Come here and hold the light, please," he said.

I hurried aboard and accepted the flash as he prepared to lean far overside.

"I think there's a body floating against the hull," he said. "Keep the light on me."

I obeyed and felt a little ill when he pulled the body out of the sea to the deck. I trained the flash on the pasty white face.

"Sam Vernon," I said.

"Yes. He's been shot. He's dead."

I had a horrible thought. "Did one of your bullets hit him?"

"No. Whoever killed him put a gun to his head and fired at extremely close range. The back of his head . . . no, I didn't kill him. Besides, he's not wearing his diving gear, so he must have come ashore somewhere and ran into—this."

I turned away and didn't look back. Murder is horrible to behold.

"We've got to report this," he said. "The best thing we can do is to bring the body to the village. Can you bear with it?"

"I'll man the wheel," I said.

Rog placed the body in my boat and I started the engine. It coughed a few times, but finally caught. I eased the craft away from the pier, opened her wide and proceeded with all possible speed down the channel to the village.

"All he's wearing are swim trunks," Rog called to me. "They must have got him as soon as he came ashore after he tried to kill you."

"If we only knew why," I called back. "Why he tried to kill me, and why someone killed him."

Rog came forward to join me at the wheel.

"What will they believe in the village?" I asked.

"It doesn't much matter."

"Yes, it does. I'm a witch, remember? I cast spells. I made Mr. Tabor ill. The moment they learn there's been a violent death, they'll blame me. This may not be Salem, but the way Tabor has these people thinking isn't far from how they believed in the old days."

"Witchcraft didn't kill Sam Vernon. Nobody will be fool enough to suggest that. Not with a hole in the back of his head. All we have to do is tell the truth." He gave me a side glance. "Up to a point."

"What point?" I asked.

"I don't think we should mention your sleeping plankton or the fact that we discovered they'd been drugged."

I looked at him in amazement. "But that's what it's all about, isn't it? Vernon's death is connected with it. Why should we hold back such information?"

"Because . . ." he hesitated. "Because I'm asking you to. You've got to trust me. Finding that narcotics are part of this business alters things so far as I'm concerned. I need time."

"Are you a police officer of some kind?" I asked bluntly.

"No."

The idea seemed ridiculous, yet I couldn't help but voice my concern. "Are you involved in this in some unlawful way?"

"My involvement is on the side of the law. That's all I can say. I need time—and your trust."

I was too tired to argue. What I wanted from Roger Randall were soft words of love, a warm embrace and a kiss. Instead, we were on a grim errand to report a murder and deliver the victim.

I said, "I'll leave the explanation of Vernon's death to you and corroborate everything you tell them."

"Thank you, Gale. I'll take over now."

138

I let him, but remained at his side, slipping my hand around his arm and resting my head on his shoulder.

He said, "If I get a break, perhaps by tomorrow I'll be able to tell you everything. The danger to you in the castle will be ended and, along with it, your distrust of me."

"But I don't distrust you," I declared vehemently.

"You do—a little. And it's understandable. You're tired, puzzled, frightened, and why shouldn't you be, with two attempts to murder you?"

"Do you think Sam Vernon was murdered because he failed to do the same to me?"

"I can't answer that yet, but I hardly think so. I think Vernon was on his own. However, you were in his way and he wanted to be rid of you. I believe whoever murdered him, wasn't interested in crude methods of disposing of you. They merely wished to frighten you away from the castle."

Rog increased the speed of the boat and we made good time. At the marina, he suggested I go to the hotel and phone the State police to report the murder. He would remain with the body. I had no desire to have any further personal contact with either Mr. or Mrs. Tabor, but I had no choice.

SIXTEEN

Much to my surprise, Mr. Tabor was behind the desk in
the lobby. He was clear-eyed and his color was good.
Certainly, he betrayed no symptoms of illness. If he was
surprised to see me, he managed to contain it well. In all
fairness, he acted swiftly once I explained my reason for
being here. He asked no questions and got on the phone
to the mainland at once. He contacted the state police and
was assured a launch would set out for the island at once.
He then phoned Horace Poole, who was the appointed
legal officer on the island. He called Dr. Baker and was
assured he'd go to the marina at once. Much to my
surprise, Mr. Tabor told me he'd accompany me back
to the marina.

Mr. Poole was well out of his element and admitted it,
stating it was the first time there'd ever been a murder on
the island. Rog related what had happened to both Mr.

Poole and Dr. Baker, with Mr. Tabor an interested listener.

It required half an hour before two state police detectives arrived. One was a lieutenant named Paul Gaylord; the other, a sergeant named Anthony Probish. Both were extremely competent.

I told my story of being adrift in my sabotaged boat; of Vernon trying to board it, armed with a knife and how I managed to prevent him from doing so. How he then rocked the boat in an attempt to pitch me into the water and how Rog had shot at him, scaring him away.

They questioned me at length then and I told them of all that had happened since I leased Witch's Castle. They took notes and Lieutenant Gaylord asked me why I'd remained there. I explained my work for my thesis and my determination to complete it. He made no comment on that, but nodded approval when Rog stated he intended to keep a close eye on me from now on.

Once they'd got all the information they wished from me, they turned their attention to Rog. He answered their questions willingly and with self-confidence.

Lieutenant Gaylord then said, "We'll have to take your rifle."

"It's not mine," Rog replied. "It was in Sam Vernon's boat. I used it to scare him away when he tried to kill Miss Dexter. But I'll be glad to relinquish it."

Lieutenant Gaylord said, "According to the doctor, it looks as if the shot was fired at close range. Even though the body was immersed in water for some time, there are still powder burns to indicate close-range shooting. Also, the bullet is still in him, so we'll soon know if this gun killed him."

"Good enough," Rog said. "The facts are simple. Sam Vernon isn't known on the island. He appeared, coming by outboard, to announce that Mr. Upton, the new owner of Witch's Castle, had sent him to landscape the property. Miss Dexter took the precaution of phoning Mr. Upton to verify this. Mr. Upton was not in his office then, but he sent word later through Mr. Tabor that he had not hired Sam Vernon and didn't know who he was."

The lieutenant asked Mr. Tabor for verification, which he readily got. He then switched his attention back to me.

"Did you tell Mr. Vernon you checked his story with Mr. Upton and found he'd lied?"

"No. As you can see, he was a big man and I was a little afraid of him."

"In view of what he attempted," the lieutenant said, "you were wise."

"We'll have him identified if he has a record of any kind," Sergeant Probish said. "That's where we'll have to start. Did you see anybody else on your end of the island?"

"No one," I said.

"It was dark when we found him," Rog explained. "Someone could have reached the island by swimming or using a rowboat. I didn't hear the sound of a motor, so I think we can eliminate the use of such a boat."

"We'll check it all out," the lieutenant promised. "Now you, Miss Dexter, live at Witch's Castle by yourself, on a lease from the former owner?"

"Yes," I said. "When the property was sold to Mr. Upton, he gave permission for me to use the house as long as necessary."

"Thank you. Mr. Randall, what are you doing on the island?"

"Frankly," Rog said, "nothing. I'm taking it easy, resting a bit. Fishing, sailing, hiking. I quit fishing after learning about Miss Dexter's observations regarding the condition of the channel waters."

"All right. We require nothing more now. As soon as

143

we identify this dead man, we'll be back. This time to take statements."

"I'll be here," I said.

"So will I," Rog assured them.

A launch was coming toward the marina at full speed, its searchlight probing the dark.

Mr. Tabor said, "That's the Mayne boat. Miss Libby must have heard the news."

It was Libby, accompanied by a man who piloted the boat but didn't come ashore. She came directly to me, her features mirroring her concern.

"I just heard the horrible news," she said. "If you're in trouble, I'm here to help."

"Thanks, Libby," I said, "but I'm not in trouble."

Rog said, "How did you hear? Only the police have been notified."

Mr. Tabor spoke up. "I also called the radio station on the mainland. I keep 'em posted if any news of importance crops up on the island."

"For a fee, I suppose," Rog said dryly.

"That's right," Mr. Tabor replied complacently.

"Is it really murder?" she asked.

Rog said, "Yes. He was shot in the back of the head."

"By whom?" she asked.

"No one knows," Rog said, "except the murderer."

"He tried to kill Miss Dexter this afternoon. Sam Vernon, that is." Surprisingly, it was Mr. Tabor who supplied the information.

I was tired and wanted to return to the castle, but since Libby had taken the trouble to come here and offer whatever help I might need, it was only fair to fill her in. I told her about my experience in the boat that afternoon. She listened intently, her expression a mixture of sympathy and shock.

While I talked, Sam Vernon's earthly remains were being transferred from my boat to the police launch.

When I finished, she pleaded with me to come back to the mainland with her, but I refused, though thanking her, and asking to be excused.

She took a small pad from her purse, wrote some numbers on a page and offered it to Rog. "This is my phone. Promise to call me if I can help Gale."

He took it and thrust it into his pocket. "Thanks, Miss Mayne. It's good to know she has a member of her own sex she can count on."

Libby touched her cheek to mine. "Go back now and get some rest. I'll keep in touch."

Rog's arm enclosed my waist and he led me to my boat and helped me aboard. Libby and Mr. Tabor stood side by side and watched as Rog eased the craft out of the slip. They waved farewell as he turned the craft to our end of the island.

The police launch left next, though veering off to head directly for the mainland. Dr. Baker and Mr. Poole accompanied the police.

Rog turned on the spotlight. He said, "Thank you, darling."

"For what?"

"Not mentioning the narcotics."

"I told you I wouldn't," I said. "Anyway, we didn't really have proof there were any narcotics involved. Now that I think about it, it's possible the debris in that drawer and on the spatula could have been some sort of headache medicine, or a cold remedy. Some of those preparations have very mild narcotics or tranquilizers. The merest trace would have affected the plankton."

His only reply was, "I'll tell you one thing. I'm grateful to those bugs of yours. I hope they wake up and live a long time."

SEVENTEEN

I wakened early, showered, dressed and was on my way
downstairs when the aroma of coffee and bacon assailed
my nostrils. I glanced in the library where Rog had
chosen to spend the night, for it had a comfortable leather
couch. There was no evidence I'd made it up for him.
The sheets and blankets had apparently already been
folded and placed in one of the drawers beneath the
bookshelves.

I continued on to the kitchen and was pleasantly surprised to see both him and Miss Mary there. She looked
like a living cameo with fair skin and black dress, sparked
with white collar and cuffs.

She greeted me with a smile and a cheery, "Good
morning, my dear. I checked your larder last night and
found it quite empty. So I brought over your breakfast."

"How nice of you." I touched my cheek to hers, for

the sight of her warmed my heart. Rog looked on with approval.

"Eggs are about done, so I suggest you sit down," he said.

"Both of you sit down," Miss Mary directed. "I've already eaten, so I'll serve."

And she did just that, allowing herself a small glass of milk and slice of toast. But, as always, she did puzzle me and sensing it, she smiled.

"I know all about the murder," she said. "I was attracted to the house last night by the electric lights reflected through the windows."

"Don't tell me you were surprised by them," I teased, referring to what she called her melding of minds.

"Not a bit," she said. "I knew you and my dear Roger had brought the body of that horrible man to the village. Not that he deserved to be murdered. Goodness knows, I deplore violence. But, with the castle empty, I was concerned about your laboratory and thought it should be guarded until you returned."

Rog gave her a sly look. "Just what would you have done had the murderer put in an appearance?"

"Charmed him," she replied matter-of-factly.

I smiled. "I believe you could."

She returned the smile. "I'm really only joking. However, I'm sure should he have put in an appearance, he'd not believe he had anything to fear in one so frail as I."

"He'd be wrong," Rog said blandly.

Miss Mary offered me the plate of bacon and eggs. "You must have more. After what you've been through, you need nourishment."

"I don't know if it's because of what I've been through," I said, "but I seem to have a voracious appetite."

"It's this beautiful, healthy air that's constantly cleansed by the sea." She offered the platter to Rog. "Eat the rest, dear."

148

"I will," he assured her and proceeded to transfer the remaining eggs and bacon to his plate.

"Have you seen any strangers on this island, Miss Mary?" I asked. "I mean, at this end."

She thought a moment. "I've caught glimpses."

"Could you identify them?" I asked.

"Not really," she said.

"Couldn't you even tell if they were male or female?" I asked, knowing she was parrying my questions.

"How can one determine sex from a distance?" she asked with feigned impatience. "The men with their long hair look like women, and the women with their pants suits and short cropped hair look like men. I haven't seen you in a dress since you came here."

"She's right," Rog said.

"I suppose," I said.

"You *know*," Miss Mary spoke with quiet firmness. "Anyway, I prefer not to get involved when I can give no definite information."

If her statement surprised me, what she said next was even more startling. She went to the stove for the coffee pot and as she was filling our cups, remarked, "But there'll be no more time for discussion. Your lovely friend from the mainland will arrive momentarily. And she'll be accompanied by two gentlemen."

Roger's eyes followed her back to the stove. "Who, Miss Mary?"

She spoke as she rejoined us. "That horrible Mr. Tabor and the new owner of this place whom I'm anxious to meet. I do hope I like him."

Roger, calmly sipping his coffee, didn't look the least bit surprised at the fact that she had identified our supposed visitors. But I'm sure I did.

"That was a very delicious breakfast," he said.

"Thank you, my dear Roger." She came over to the table and planted a kiss on his brow.

"I enjoyed it too, Miss Mary, and I appreciate your bringing it."

"And cooking it," Roger said. He stood up, put an arm around her and pressed her head gently to his chest. "I think I'm going to have to adopt you."

She laughed happily. "It's the other way around. I've adopted you. Both of you, since you're so obviously in love. And since you are, it's Gale you should be embracing."

He laughed, kissed her brow, then came over to me. He tilted my chin, bent down and was about to kiss me when Miss Mary interrupted.

"It will have to wait, I'm afraid," she said. "Our friends are almost here."

Rog kissed me anyway, then helped me from the chair. The sound of a motor was now evident.

"Let's see what they want," Rog said, leading the way.

"Please come, Miss Mary," I said, extending a hand. She placed hers in it, gave me a grateful smile and we followed Rog. Our visitors were already on the porch when he opened the door. Rog didn't appear the least bit surprised to see the three Miss Mary had already stated were on their way, but I was. I couldn't make up my mind whether she was playing a game with me, or whether she really did have a gift of looking into the future.

We exchanged greetings and I invited them into the living room. Rog touched a match to the paper in the fireplace and we took seats around it. Rog remained standing, his attention on the kindling, already igniting.

"May I offer you some coffee?" I asked, after I'd made the introductions.

"No, thanks," Libby said. "I already breakfasted at the inn with Mr. Upton."

"He's the new owner of the castle," I told Miss Mary.

"Witch's Castle," he replied, smiling. "I'm fascinated by the name."

"I am not," Miss Mary said primly. "The designation refers to the original owner, Sarah Dexter, for whom I have great admiration."

Mr. Tabor said, "You're the only one that has."

"No, she isn't," Rog said. "I've seen Sarah Dexter's portrait. She was gorgeous."

"I agree," I said. "Quite a lady."

"I'll go along with that," Libby said. "Miss Mary told me about her the day she kindly invited me in to lunch."

Miss Mary said, "I knew the three of you were coming and I'd have flagged you down for coffee, except I had to come over here with breakfast. Gale is so much the scientist, she forgets about food."

Libby looked puzzled. "Strange you should say that, since Mr. Upton had no intention of coming out here. We met at the inn. I breakfasted there because I didn't want to arrive too early. I couldn't sleep last night thinking about Gale here alone."

"I'm sorry," I said, "because I slept beautifully. Perhaps because I was so exhausted."

Miss Mary said, "I think I'd sleep too if I'd had to fight off a murderer."

Mr. Upton said, "I presume you're a resident, Miss Selwich."

"Oh yes," she replied serenely. "But please call me Miss Mary. Everyone does—except when they call me Crazy Mary."

He looked startled. "Why would anyone do that?"

"Ask Mr. Tabor," she said.

Mr. Upton's glance flicked to Tabor, who looked uncomfortable under Miss Mary's placid gaze.

"Tell him, Mr. Tabor," she said.

"Well," he said, coloring slightly, "it's just that the villagers really believe Sarah Dexter was a witch. They

151

steer clear of this house 'cause strange things have happened here. Voices been heard, furniture moves, even the castle is supposed to have moved. You check with former owners, Mr. Upton, you'll find out I'm tellin' the truth."

I hoped he wouldn't ask me about it, for I'd have to admit Mr. Tabor's statement was accurate.

Mr. Upton said, "But what does that have to do with the villagers' antagonism toward this gentle lady?"

"She likes the castle," Tabor said. "She reveres the memory of the wit . . . Sarah Dexter."

Mr. Upton said, "I like her the better for it."

"Thank you, Mr. Upton." Miss Mary brushed an imaginary piece of lint from her black skirt and let her hands rest, palms upward, demurely in her lap. "I will never allow anyone to revile the memory of Sarah Dexter in my presence. What they do behind my back, I have no control over, any more than I can prevent the villagers from calling me Crazy Mary."

"No one had better make such a statement in my presence," he said.

Rog addressed Mr. Upton. "The young people on the island and those who come here for the summer have a deep affection for Miss Mary. I might add, I have also."

"And I," I said.

"I think we're unanimous then," Mr. Upton said, "and that brings us to the business at hand. First of all, I want to thank Miss Mayne for giving me a lift."

"It was the least I could do," she replied. "You bought my breakfast."

He went on, "The police phoned me last night to notify me of the murder which could have occurred on my property. They wanted to know if I was acquainted with Sam Vernon. I'd never heard of the man. Contrary to what he told you, Miss Dexter, he never approached me about working here. In view of what I learned from the

152

police after I flew up here, I'm not surprised our paths never crossed."

"What did they learn about Vernon?" Rog spoke as he put two medium-sized logs on the fire.

"Vernon has a long record which includes everything from burglary, armed robbery, numerous assaults and even drug peddling in a small way. It's their opinion he was the victim of revenge. He'd double-crossed his pals before. This time, he paid for it with his life."

Tabor said, "The bullet came from a thirty-eight. That clears you, Mr. Randall."

"I still don't think Gale should stay here," Libby said worriedly. "Please come back with me."

"I'm not afraid, now that Vernon is no longer here. And I really can't leave my work. My whole future depends on it."

"If you stay here, you may not have one," Libby said.

"I will stay with you, my dear," Miss Mary said.

"I hardly think you'd scare away a murderer." Mr. Upton softened his statement with a smile. "If he's still about."

I didn't want to say I wasn't alone, since Rog had spent the night on the couch in the library and would continue to do so. It would be the type of gossip Mr. Tabor would love to bring back to the village. I noticed Rog also remained silent. He too knew the way Mr. Tabor's mind worked.

Mr. Upton arose, walked over to the fire and extended his hands toward its warmth. I didn't blame him. The temperature in the room couldn't have been any more than in the mid-fifties.

"I'm afraid my reason for coming concerns you, Miss Dexter."

"In what way, Mr. Upton?" I asked.

He turned to face me. "As you know, when I talked

153

with you at the inn, I told you the castle was yours for as long as you felt the need for it."

"And I appreciated your kindness," I said, hoping to fend off what I felt was coming.

"Well"—his smile was apologetic—"at the time, I didn't realize the villagers were so antagonistic toward you. But there's been a murder committed here and that's changed things."

"In what way?" Rog asked.

"The murderer could still be around here. He might even be a native—an islander."

"Why would an islander wish to kill Sam Vernon?" I asked. "Nobody here knew him."

"So far as anyone knows," Mr. Upton replied. "But your name is the same as that of the first owner of the castle. There's been no trouble on the island—no previous murder. There's talk in the village about burning this place down. I just bought it and you can't blame me for wanting to protect my investment."

"Of course I don't," I replied. "But I can't believe the villagers would do that."

"My dear," Miss Mary broke into the conversation, "a mob came here to do away with Sarah Dexter."

"That was over a hundred years ago," I protested. "Surely . . ."

"A mob is a mob," Rog said. "Whether a hundred years ago or today. Play on their emotions and anything could happen. I think Mr. Upton is correct. If the murderer is a villager, what better way for him to divert suspicion from himself than to stir up a mob against you."

Mr. Upton said, "That's what I fear. I'll not order you out, Miss Dexter. However, I am asking you, as a favor, to please leave the premises."

"But all my equipment is here," I argued.

Rog said, "I'll keep an eye on the place to see that no one enters."

I was shocked that he was so completely in agreement with Mr. Upton. But I'd not give up so easily.

"There is no other place on this island I can stay," I said.

"You could stay with me, my dear," Miss Mary said.

"I appreciate the offer, Miss Mary, but then you'd be in danger."

Mr. Upton said, "You can stay at the inn."

"Mr. Tabor would never permit that," I said smugly.

"Yes, I would, Miss Dexter," he replied. "I know I wasn't nice to you, but I'll open a room so you can stay there 'til you get what you call your work completed. That's the reason I came out here."

"What's the difference if I stay at the inn or at the castle?"

Mr. Upton's smile was embarrassed. "I'll compromise. I don't want my property destroyed, but I don't think you'd be bothered coming here in the daytime. But to stay overnight—to live here—I'd rather you didn't. As a favor to me."

"I guess I have no choice."

"You'd better go upstairs and pack, dear," Miss Mary said, as if the matter were settled—which it was. "I'll clean up in the kitchen."

I turned my attention to Mr. Tabor. "You had a rapid recovery. May I take credit for that, since you blamed me for the illness?"

His face flamed. "Guess it was just an upset stomach. I got an ulcer and when you got uppity about my mentionin' your being related to Sarah Dexter, I got real upset."

I wanted to say I had also, but I'd had enough talk of witch's tales.

Libby said, "May I give you a lift back to the inn?"

Rog said, "I'd like the privilege of bringing Gale to the village. That is, if she'll loan me her boat."

I was irked with him for not having taken sides with me, but not so much that I didn't wish to be in his company. Besides, I thought, perhaps he was right. I'd be safer at the inn. At least, I hoped I would.

After Libby, Mr. Upton and Mr. Tabor left, Rog went to his cottage. Miss Mary returned to the kitchen after refusing my help and I went upstairs to pack. I was heartsick at the turn things had taken and wondered if I'd ever complete the work for my thesis. It seemed as if powerful forces were working to prevent me from doing so. At least it was a challenge, I told myself, and one I'd meet head on.

Yet could I, by myself? Certainly, if Rog hadn't shot at Sam Vernon yesterday to frighten him away, I'd not be alive now. I thrust that thought from my mind and turned to my packing. I'd just completed it when Rog returned. He came upstairs for my bags and brought them to the boat. I said my farewells to Miss Mary, who cupped my face between her hands and assured me she'd keep an eye on my laboratory. I thanked her and ran down to the dock where Rog awaited me.

We cruised at a moderate speed and I basked in the bright sunlight and warming temperatures.

"Do you trust Mr. Tabor?" I asked.

"I've just about decided not to trust anybody," he said.

"Not even Miss Mary?" I teased.

He laughed. "She's a doll. Yes, I trust her. Don't you?"

"I'm both enchanted and bewildered by her. She's certainly gifted with a sixth sense."

"Apparently," he said. "Probably it comes from living alone so much. I don't mean she's senile or gifted with lucky guessing. I don't know what I mean exactly. But she's definitely *not* on my list of suspects."

"Rog, why did you want me out of the castle?"

"It was Upton who wanted you out."

"You didn't seem to mind."

"All right, Gale. I guess you have a right to know what I'm concerned about."

"Thanks for saying that. You *can* trust me, you know."

His arm enclosed my shoulders and tightened gently. "I know that, darling. Now what I'm about to tell you is mere suspicion. Remember that. But should I be right, you could, by living in the castle, be in danger. Let's keep in mind a murder was committed. Also, the murderer is still loose."

"I know all that," I said impatiently. "What I don't know is how the castle is, in some way, connected with the murder of Sam Vernon. And it is, isn't it?"

"I think so. Now, mind you, this is mere supposition. But I suspect Witch's Castle has been used for years as a narcotics drop. It's brought from Europe, Marseilles probably, and carried here by private boat. Somewhere along the coast it's thrown overside in special waterproof and tideproof containers. These are later picked up and brought to the castle. The stuff is then cut and packaged for distribution. The castle has been vacant for years, except for two or three occasions when Mr. Abrams rented it for the owners. The people stayed briefly and fled. So long as these drug peddlers and smugglers could keep the castle a place which no one would visit, they felt safe. They did that by scaring away not only those who rented it, but those who bought it. Only you didn't scare so easily."

"I scared," I said firmly. "It's my work which has kept me there. It's still going to."

"Perhaps, so long as you occupy it only during the day, they won't object," Rog said grimly. "Though I still don't like you there."

"I think I'll be lazy today," I said. "Not that I want to be, but if someone here is involved—and someone likely is—it will probably allay their suspicions."

157

Rog looked relieved. "I'm in favor of that, but I'll tell you what I'm going to do tomorrow. Do some diving."

The news excited me. "I've a dry suit at the castle. May I go along? I want to get some samples of mud and aquatic life."

"Why not? I'll pick you up at the marina at seven."

"I'll be there," I said enthusiastically.

He regarded me curiously. "Why didn't you bring everything to the inn?"

"Because I have every intention of returning to the castle."

We'd reached the marina then and he escorted me to the hotel. He had to make a second trip, since I'd brought the same number of bags I'd left with, though some contained only books. If he guessed, he made no comment. Our farewell in the lobby was formal under Mr. Tabor's watchful gaze. But I had to admit I was treated with genuine courtesy, and when I asked to put through a call to my parents, he was most cooperative. I knew the news of the murder was in the paper, and no doubt the history of the castle and its name would be played up. I wanted to reassure my parents I was involved in no danger. It would be no lie as, while I was at the inn, I didn't feel I would be.

EIGHTEEN

Rog was awaiting me when I reached the marina. He maneuvered the boat out of the slot and set it on its course.

He said, "It's a good thing that deep-sea diving is part of your work. It means we can dive without arousing suspicion. If I'm right, those concerned won't realize we suspect the reason behind this violence and danger is drugs."

"I hope you're right. As for our diving, the first time I checked into the hotel, I told Mr. Tabor that it would be a large part of my work."

"Good. We'll get to it as soon as we get back. Weather reports hint about a possible blow by nightfall and no prediction how long it will last, so we'd best cover as much of the ocean bottom as possible today."

"Mind telling me what you're looking for?"

"Officially, I'm helping you," he said, smiling. "Unofficially, I'm not sure. But I have a feeling there's something down there Sam Vernon knew about. He went after it and was murdered."

"Do you think Perry Tabor is involved?"

"He's certainly kept close tabs on you."

"What about Mr. Upton?"

"He seems okay. I've heard of him—a businessman with a good reputation and out to protect his interests. You can't blame him for that."

"I don't."

"Don't you think Libby Mayne has taken an unusual interest in your welfare?"

"Good heavens," I exclaimed. "You suspect her?"

"Why not? Her father runs a factory producing many kinds of chemicals. It employs a number of chemists. He could use the castle to cut the narcotics. He'd be in a position to have many outlets through which he could channel the final product."

"I hope you're wrong," I said. "I like Libby. It would hurt to learn she was using me."

"I might be one hundred percent wrong. That's why I want to do some diving, and the quicker we get to it, the better."

Rog insisted on going up to the castle with me and inspecting the entire place. I made some quick checks on my supplies and on the progress of several experiments I had going. Rog returned to the kitchen, assuring me the place seemed not to have been occupied, though he scolded me for having left so many of my clothes.

"It's a dead give-away you intend to come back," he said.

"It might also convince them I'm completely unaware that things here are not as innocent as they seem."

"I'll not start the day by arguing with the woman I

love." He kissed me briefly, then left to change, adding that he'd return as soon as he was ready.

I hadn't used my suit since spring, but I'd packed it carefully, dusted it well with talcum so the rubber surfaces wouldn't stick. I found it to be in excellent condition.

I liked the dry type of suit, which utilized dead air between the layers as insulation against cold. Here, at this season of the year I'd need it, for the water was frigid.

I donned long underwear first and then got into the rubber suit without trouble. I put my tank and face mask, flippers and weight belt on the back porch. When I went out, Rog was there, dressed in a similar suit. I left him on the porch while I returned to the laboratory in the kitchen, and came back with collection bottles, a plankton net and a curved, hoe-like tool with which to uproot plant life intact.

We carried everything out to the pier and completed our dress. The hood and face mask went on last. Roger went to the end of the pier, nodded and then slipped into the water, feet first. I eased myself off the side of the pier and dropped.

I memorized the time on my watch because time was an important factor in these waters at this season. I felt none of the cold, for the suit was highly efficient, but after a certain time I would, and before that happened, I must be out of the water.

I saw Rog near the bottom. The sea was shallow here, but deep enough so we swam out side by side. I towed my collecting equipment and I was genuinely interested in obtaining samples for laboratory examination.

We reached deeper water where the light didn't penetrate as well, so we continued to remain close together, following the rule that a diver must always be accompanied by another diver.

161

I didn't know what we were searching for, but I suspected any sort of article on the bottom which looked like a container. I also watched for likely places where there'd be small mounds of mud indicating sea worms were hidden inside these. I wanted specimens of the larger varieties.

From time to time, he signaled directions and I followed them. We were covering a fairly large part of the ocean bottom and striking well out beyond the pier. We had to remain close to the bottom and visibility grew less and less, though we could make out one another well enough so far.

I spotted an area of small mounds and I kicked my way to the bottom where I used my hoe-like tool to dig deeply into one mound. I found the worms I wanted, stuffed them into one of my jars, got the lid back on successfully and then I hunted for plants. Often they grew in the vicinity of these worm colonies, so I moved slowly, checking anything that looked interesting.

Suddenly I realized that I'd lost sight of Rog. We couldn't stay in the water much longer, so I began swimming close to the surface where the light was better and where I hoped I might spot him.

I saw the dark mass moving below me and I felt reassured. I dived again and swam toward him. The sun was higher now and there was more light, even at this depth. I waved to him and held up a specimen bottle to show him I'd found what I wanted. He began swimming closer to me.

He was holding a spear gun and continued to move in my direction. Suddenly my sense of relief was shattered by the fact that Rog had not been in possession of a spear gun and couldn't possibly have had time to swim back and procure one. Besides, this was a type of gun using a blank cartridge for power, to send the spear at a victim with speed and accuracy that rubber-propelled guns could not achieve. I'd seen these at Woods Hole when students were after species of marine life that moved too fast for a conventional weapon.

As I watched, the man in the wet suit raised the gun. He was aiming it at me. I kicked violently to propel myself out of the way. The gun moved to keep me in its sights. I dived for the bottom. If that failed and he came after me, I'd have to surface, but that would be the most dangerous move of all because the closer we got to the surface, the plainer I'd become and a better target.

I had one thing in my favor. I knew this type of gun and it was a single shot. When he fired the spear, he'd not have another chance. Not with the gun, but he no doubt had a knife and he'd be after me with that.

I flashed by him and I saw the spear unloosened. I gave a savage twist of my body, swam to the left, dived again. Nothing ripped into my suit or my flesh, so the spear had missed, but the unidentified diver was still a great menace.

I wondered where Rog was and I found myself hoping he was not close by, for if he innocently approached this murderer, Rog might not be as lucky as I.

My flippers touched bottom and I gave a mighty kick to take me toward the surface before the murderer discovered where I was. My head broke the water. I looked around in panic and saw no one. Nor was there any sign of a boat. The mysterious diver could have reached the point from anywhere on the island, and swam back there without being seen. I hoped that was what he was doing at this moment.

Another mask-enclosed head popped into view. I didn't wait to see if it was Rog or the would-be murderer. I struck out for the pier, luckily not too far away. I knew the other diver was behind me and coming up quite fast. He suddenly turned over to float, showing me that he meant no harm. He began to swim slowly, not trying to overtake me. I still kept well ahead of him. If the diver was Rog, no harm was being done except, possibly, to puzzle him sorely. If it was the man who'd been intent on taking my life, I was safer staying away from him.

I reached the pier and hauled myself out of the water. I kicked off the flippers, removed my face mask, prepared to run. The man who came out of the water was now recognizable and I knew it was Rog. He stripped off his mask as he reached the pier.

"What's the matter?" he asked.

"There was another diver—with a spear gun. One of those Thunderbolt powder types . . . he shot at me."

Rog said, "Get in the boat."

I clambered aboard and started the engine. He pulled himself over the side and crouched near the rail, his mask once again in place. He peered down through the water as I sent the boat moving out to greater depths.

He perched himself on the rail and continued his search. Suddenly he slid, feet first, in the water and vanished. I kept cruising around the immediate area. Ten minutes passed before he surfaced. He crawled aboard and removed his mask.

"Nothing," he said. "I thought I saw something when I dived, but it could have been a big fish. Were you able to see what he looked like?"

"No. He wore a full mask just as we did. I thought it was you until I was lucky enough to notice that he had this spear gun and you were not carrying one. Lucky too, it was a single shot."

"Keep cruising around," Rog suggested. "He might have to surface for some reason, though I doubt it."

"Why did he try to kill me?" I asked.

"I don't think he knew who you were, except that you must be looking for the same thing he was. I'm going

164

down again. You stay with the boat. Maybe I'll get lucky and find what we're all apparently searching for."

He slid overside. I began to circle slowly, watching apprehensively for any trace of the mysterious diver. If the stranger came upon Rog suddenly, he might have the advantage of surprise. I was prepared to stop the engine, throw out the sea anchor and dive myself if I saw him.

Rog surfaced and I helped him aboard. He shook his head. "Nothing. He's gone. Let's go back."

I piloted the boat to the pier and tied it up. We returned to the castle where I changed into slacks and towel-dried my hair. Then I set up the laboratory for testing the samples I'd brought from the bottom.

Rog was seated on the porch, basking in the noonday sun, when I joined him. The sunlight felt good after being in the chilly water so long. For the first time in hours, I relaxed, until the burned-out hulk of my car reminded me that we were still in a great deal of danger.

"Could you tell if it was a man or woman in the diving suit?" he asked.

I knew he was referring to Libby. "No," I said. "I was in too much of a hurry to get out of the area."

He was holding my hand and he squeezed it gently. "You did the right thing. Anyway, it assures us our suspicions aren't unfounded. After I rest and get a little more sun, I'm going back on the water. He'll probably come back, and when he does, there'll undoubtedly be a fast boat somewhere close by to come out and pick up whatever the diver finds. If it was weighted to stay put on the bottom, it'll be too heavy for him to tow ashore, so a boat will be necessary."

The sun slipped behind clouds, ending the warmth we'd been basking in. I said, "Before I came out, I noticed the barometer was falling fast. The storm is coming closer. You can feel the weather changing."

165

He nodded and glanced skyward. The sky was gradually becoming layered with clouds and a grayness that portended a storm.

He said, "I'll take you back to the village immediately."

"I'm not going back."

"Yes, you are. It's too dangerous for you here now. There've been three attempts on your life. I think they've decided to throw caution to the winds. They want no further interference or interruptions. Your presence is a nuisance to them."

"What about yours?" I countered.

"I'm a man," he said. "At least the odds aren't as great."

"I'm staying," I said. "I'm sick and tired of this business of witches, moaning houses, screams and voices calling on Satan. There's just one way we can force the hand of whoever is behind this. Make him show himself. The best way is for me to once again take occupancy of this house."

"It's a terrible risk."

"One I'm willing to take."

He arose, drew me up and took me in his arms. "Gale, please—let me take you back to the village."

"No," I said firmly. "Anyway, I've work to do. My life from the sea won't remain alive forever."

I slipped from his arms and went back into the house. Once inside the door, I turned.

He was regarding me, stern-faced. "I love you in spite of your stubbornness. But did you ever stop to think that your staying here makes my task harder? Besides trying to snoop around, I've got to guard you too?"

I smiled. "I have a good pair of lungs. If a killer shows up, I'll scream to high heaven."

"A lot of good that will do you if I'm out on the water with the motor running."

I laughed. "Good luck. I'm going to work."

I blew him a kiss and closed the door. Alone, I didn't feel quite as brave as I'd pretended, but I wasn't going to leave him here by himself. I was as aware of the gravity of the situation as he, and while I didn't know what I could do if the enemy showed himself, I'd certainly do my best to give a good account of myself.

NINETEEN

Rog stopped by on his way to the pier. He was once again wearing his diving suit and also a rifle. I suggested he take time for lunch, but he refused, stating he was anxious to get back on the water and cruise about, hoping for a glimpse of the mysterious diver. He had his helmet and tanks so he'd be ready to dive in less than a minute.

I went to work, examining the specimens I'd just taken from the sea. Microscopic work indicated the bottom plant life was not healthy. My collection of sea worms seemed active enough, but when I fixed them, froze portions of them in wax and sliced them into tissue-thin pieces with a microtome, I detected, under the high power, the changes made in their bodies by pollution. They were an important source of food for fish, which, in turn, would absorb the poison and soon die.

I made my notes, set up the analytical test for mercury

salts, and made my entries; I had all I needed. The evidence was now perfectly clear that taking edible sea life from these waters was unwise, and the sale of them had to be stopped. Also, sports fishermen providing seafood for their families had to be warned.

My work was done. From my notes, I could now write my thesis. I no longer had an excuse to remain here. Yet, I couldn't let Rog face danger alone. I felt a sense of accomplishment. The work I'd done had been painstaking and I hoped it would be well received. I thought about mailing the information to a government agency, but I decided against this until I could talk to Libby. Though Rog mentioned her as a suspect in connection with this narcotics business—for which he admitted he had no positive evidence—I still trusted her.

In mid-afternoon, I heard the approach of a car and saw by the signal lights and siren atop it, that it was the state police. Apparently, they'd come to take statements from me and Rog. I went out to welcome them and saw Rog, cruising slowly in the channel. He must have either heard or observed the car, for he turned the boat around, picking up speed on his way back.

Only Lieutenant Gaylord was in the car. When I admitted him, he looked about with interest.

"So this is Witch's Castle," he said. "As a kid, I conjured all sorts of spooks living in it and I expected something gloomy. It's downright cheerful."

"Made so, no doubt, by recent owners."

"It didn't keep them here though," he observed. "Aren't you frightened? Even if the place hadn't been christened Witch's Castle, it's lonely. Besides, with all that's happened to you since you moved here, I should think you'd pack up and go."

"I will—very soon," I said. "My work is about completed."

I made no mention of the incident of a few hours ago

170

when there'd been another attempt on my life by a diver with a lethal spear. It was enough that Rog knew about it. Also, I feared the lieutenant might insist on my leaving.

"What did you find out about the water?" the lieutenant asked.

"The kindest thing I can say is, don't fish there until it's cleared up."

He whistled sharply. "Nobody around here's going to like *that*."

"I know, but they must be told."

"I suggest you keep it quiet until after you're out of this house."

"Don't tell me you've heard rumors they're going to burn the place down because of me."

He spoke with a quiet firmness. "Not just rumors, Miss Dexter. Statements of fact. We don't want trouble. The people here are good. It's just that fishing is their livelihood."

"I know," I replied patiently. "That's why it's so important for those who are polluting these waters, to stop."

"You're referring to the plant on the mainland."

"I am. And Miss Mayne has assured me her father is already at work on it."

Lieutenant Gaylord sighed. "I wish it could be done overnight."

"So do I," I said. "But it must be done quickly. May I tempt you with a cup of coffee?"

"You sure can," he said, sniffing appreciatively.

"I just perked it. Come on out to the kitchen."

"Glad to. Give me a chance to see the place."

I poured two cups and I saw him regarding my lab bench curiously. While we sipped the coffee, I explained the workings of some of the apparatus. I was pleased at his interest and his questions. I then switched our conversation to the legend of the castle.

"Tell me, Lieutenant, did you grow up hearing the story of Sarah Dexter?"

"Yes," he replied. "I was born here. However, I never believed in witchcraft and thought the whole thing was pretty silly, except for the part where the woman vanished. That was tragic."

"What do you think happened to her?"

"I always had an idea she took a boat to sea to avoid the mob that came out here to do away with her. Probably fell overboard and drowned. Anyway, there was never a trace of her."

"It's sad," I said. "I wonder if she was ever mourned."

"Probably not by anyone but Miss Mary. She reveres Sarah Dexter's memory."

I smiled. "I'm glad to hear you refer to her as Miss Mary."

He chuckled. "She's a real cutie. Gentle as a summer breeze, but always gets her own way and makes you like giving it to her."

"You know, of course, the villagers believe I'm a descendant of Sarah Dexter."

"Are you?"

"Not that I know of. More coffee?"

"Please."

I filled his cup. "Just what is the story told about Sarah Dexter and her disappearance?"

"Usual stuff told about so-called witches. They claimed she caused milk to sour as it was taken from the herds. That dogs sickened and died, and that children grew ill because she hated their parents. They even attributed poor fishing seasons to her, until it got to the point where they decided she was a menace and came out to lynch her. They found candles lit, food cooking on the stove, doors open—but Sarah had vanished. They said she caused herself to be transported to a safer place and she never came back. Not until three or four years ago."

"I heard nothing about that," I said.

"Well, it wasn't much anyway. The house had stood idle for years. From time to time, folks bought it, but never would live there for long. Their stories were the same—that Sarah Dexter was back. Or had never left. A few made formal complaints at the barracks or to the local police on the mainland. Their stories were investigated, but nothing was found to substantiate their claims."

"I presume you met the new owner."

"Had to call him about the murder and met him yesterday when he flew up. He was upset about the publicity and, of course, the murder."

"I'm sure he was, but then so was I."

He glanced out the window. "Looks like it's setting for a good blow. You know, speaking of witchcraft, there was one strange thing connected with this house. As you probably know, we get frequent summer storms. Anyway, a couple of former owners stayed four or five days and then left. I got to wondering why some lasted one night, others a few days. I discovered one thing in common. Those who left fast spent the night here during a storm. Those who stayed had fair weather until the night before they cleared out, when it also stormed. So it seems Sarah comes back on the winds of the storm. It may be a coincidence, but it happened almost too often to be that."

The door opened, admitting Rog. He was still wearing his diving suit and he looked cold. "Hello, Lieutenant. It's beginning to blow."

"How about some coffee?" I asked. "It's still hot."

He rubbed his hands briskly, stirring up circulation. "The way I feel, I could drink it straight from the pot."

I poured him a large mug. He cupped his hands around it, warming them.

Lieutenant Gaylord set down his empty mug. "I haven't stated my real reason for coming here. I want a further statement from both of you about finding the man you know as Sam Vernon."

"What was his real name?" Rog asked.

"Tony Moffitt. He had a long record of drug peddling. In later years, he arose above that to become part of a syndicate that imported drugs by the kilo. There's little question in our minds but that he was murdered by other drug merchants whom he quite likely double-crossed. He was noted for it."

So, I thought, Rog's hunch was right. There was a connection with the illicit narcotics traffic. I wondered how he'd ever guessed it so accurately.

For the next hour, we gave the Lieutenant our stories and then signed the statements he wrote by hand. When we accompanied him to his car, all three of us looked at the darkening sky.

"This," Lieutenant Gaylord mused, "is going to be a doozer. I'd better get going. The ferry doesn't operate in bad storms. Thanks again for your cooperation and the coffee, Miss Dexter."

We watched him pull away, then turned back to the house.

Rog said, "I'll retrieve my gear from the boat and take it to my cottage. Be back after I change."

I said, "Miss Mary brought two steaks and potatoes, already baked. I'll cream them and broil the steaks."

"I'll be ready for them," he called back.

By the time he returned, the wind was already blowing hard and whistling its way into a full-fledged storm. Rog warned that, since the power came from the village and the poles he'd put up were flimsy, chances were the wiring would blow down. I brought out lamps and candles, just in case.

I touched a match to the paper in the library fireplace and stood there watching it burn and ignite the kindling. Rog had placed small logs atop the kindling and I let them catch before I put on a larger one. There was a square table of medium size, covered with a lace cloth, which set before a window. I brought it over and placed it before the fireplace. On it, I put a pewter candelabra in which were two slender candles.

I set two places, then returned to the kitchen to prepare the dinner. I creamed the potatoes and added cheese which Miss Mary had also thoughtfully provided; from some fresh fruit I made a salad. The steaks were large, so I felt we'd have enough. I knew we would, when Rog returned with a pint of ice cream from his freezer. That, along with coffee, made an elegant dinner.

The setting was romantic and the fireplace gave off a warmth that prompted me to run upstairs at the last minute and slip into the blouse and long skirt I'd brought. Thank goodness I'd not packed it. I pinned a cameo to the high neck and I felt very nineteenth century.

When I came downstairs, Rog already had the dinner on the table. He cried out in surprise at sight of me, and gathered me into his arms.

"Just looking at you blots out the crazy wild wind and the driving rain," he said. "Only you shouldn't look so helpless and beautiful. I'll not be able to concentrate on dinner."

"Please try, at least. It's simple, but I put my best efforts into it."

He kissed me briefly, then released me. "Well, since you cooked the dinner, okay. Otherwise, I'd say forget it."

"Liar," I joshed. "You know you're starved and so am I."

He seated me, kissed the tip of my nose, then took his seat.

I said, "I wish Miss Mary were here to enjoy it with us."

"Ordinarily I'd agree, because I'd love to have her

see you, but tonight I'll not share you. You look so lady-like, you make me dizzy."

Our conversation throughout the meal was equally foolish, but it was the talk of two people in love . . . the slightest nonsensical statement sent us into gales of laughter.

Not until we were back in the kitchen, did Rog notice my laboratory stripped down and most of the equipment packed in cartons.

"So you're leaving," he commented.

"That's problematical. But my work here is completed. Lieutenant Gaylord asked me not to make my findings known here until after I was gone."

"Will you?"

"That depends on what I learn from Libby. I intend to stop in at the factory before I go. But I'm not going until you do."

"I don't know when I'll be going," Rog said. "But I'll be happy to see you get off this island."

"What are your plans?" I asked.

"Tomorrow, if the storm is over, I'm going to do more diving."

"I'm going with you," I said.

"Too dangerous."

"For one it would be. Together, we can keep an eye on each other."

His sigh was one of exasperation. "Why are you so stubborn?"

I ignored his question to ask one of my own. "Can you tell me now just what your work is?"

"Believe it or not, I'm in the insurance business."

"Why haven't you tried to sell me a policy?" I teased.

But he wasn't in the mood for joking. "I didn't say I sold insurance and I can't go into detail just now."

"Okay," I said. "No more questions. If we're going to dive tomorrow morning, I think we'd better get some rest."

"Agreed. Miss Mary put my bedclothes in the drawer on the far side of the fireplace." He grinned. "They'll be warm anyway."

"No need to make up the couch," I said matter-of-factly. "You're not staying."

He pushed his chair back and stood up. "I have half a mind to tie you onto the back of my motorbike and take you to the village and when the ferry makes its first trip, put you on it and ship you back to the mainland."

"I don't blame you." I started gathering up the dishes and placing them on the tray I'd used to bring in our dinner. "But I'll not leave the castle until the mystery of the voice and the shrieks and moans are explained."

"Have you forgotten three attempts were made on your life?"

"No. Why didn't you tell Lieutenant Gaylord about the last one?"

"Why didn't you?" he countered.

"I wasn't sure you'd want me to."

He looked away.

I said, "You didn't, did you?"

"No, I didn't," he retorted. "If the police start cruising these waters, I'll never get away from here."

I knew he meant the police would scare away whoever had an interest in this place—or something it contained.

"I figured you'd not want it known."

"That doesn't mean I want you killed," he said impatiently.

I picked up the tray, but he took it from me and headed for the kitchen, with me following.

"Rog, has it ever occurred to you that you and I have been very selfish?"

He set the tray down on the kitchen table with a clatter and spun around. "What the hell are you talking about?"

"Just this. And please hear me out. Miss Mary comes here often. She keeps this place up herself. She even dresses in gowns she's found in the trunks in the attic.

"What are you getting at?"

"Miss Mary considers this castle hers. She doesn't want anyone in it. Whoever is behind the violence and murder which has occurred here, doesn't want anyone in it either."

"Miss Mary." He spoke her name reverently. Our eyes met in a look of complete understanding.

I said, "She could be murdered in this house and the superstitious islanders would attribute it to Sarah Dexter. Miss Mary can't fight those men."

"You can't either," he replied. "But your idea is to draw them into the open."

I nodded. "They'll be annoyed when they learn or see—if they're snooping around—I'm back in the castle."

"At least," Rog said thoughtfully, "I'll stand guard outside."

"No, you won't," I replied.

"I can't let you stay in here alone overnight," he replied vehemently.

"You can and you will," I said. "Please, darling. It's the only way."

"Suppose they come," he said.

"I have a healthy pair of lungs."

"How will I hear you with the wind and rain?"

"I'll be locked in my bedroom," I replied. "Don't worry. All they want to do is scare me away from here."

"They've taken cute ways of doing it, haven't they?"

I ignored his sarcasm. "Now, run along."

"Can't I even help with the dishes?" He looked uneasy at the thought of leaving me here.

I smiled. "Nope. I feel quite unafraid."

He took me in his arms. "You look beautiful. That alone is reason enough for me to stay."

"Thanks, my love. I'll walk you to the door."

"You're heartless," he said. "A beautiful fire still

178

flaming in the library fireplace, the setting ideal for making love, and you send me home."

"The quicker we solve this puzzle, the quicker we can both leave—then we'll make love."

"By the way," he asked suddenly. "Will you marry me?"

"If you leave at once," I said.

For answer, he kissed me with a passionate abandon that left me breathless. I returned the embrace, wondering how I could bear to be separated from him ever again. This time, it was he who released me.

His voice was gruff as he said, "Good night, you foolish, exciting, lovable, exasperating woman."

He went out the back door. I knew it was because he felt that if he walked even the distance through the castle to the front, he might change his mind and not go. If he had, I wondered if I'd have had the willpower to send him back to his cottage.

Now that he was gone, the quiet and loneliness of the castle seemed to close in on me, and I knew my plan had been a reckless one. I'm sure he knew it too, but I could think of no faster way of our leaving this place. I wanted us both away from here, so we'd be free to start a life of our own. But I knew I couldn't do it with a clear conscience, with Miss Mary coming here. It was only during our dinner hour, when I was so happy, I thought of her. I wondered if, in her mind's eye, she had visualized Rog and me before the fireplace, glorying in the wonder of our love.

TWENTY

I had just finished putting away the dishes when the lights went out. Whether the storm had caused a power failure or whether the poles Rog had erected for the wiring had been blown down, I didn't know. But since he'd warned me about it, I wasn't frightened. It was an inconvenience, but one I could cope with. I'd dropped a packet of matches into my skirt pocket at the time we got out the candles and lamps, so I lit a match and applied its flame to two lamp wicks.

As always, the sight of my microscope proved irresistible. I slipped off the cover, retrieved a couple of slides from the carton in which I'd packed them and studied plankton forms for almost three hours, learning still more about them. It was only fatigue that made me aware of the time.

I covered the microscope, washed the slides and repacked the instruments I'd used. I put out one lamp, carried the other as I checked both back and front doors, turning the bolt in each. I checked the windows to make certain no panes of glass had been broken by the savage winds. The fireplace in the library showed only a few embers glowing, and I used the poker to scatter them, so they'd die faster. My chores on this floor completed, I went upstairs. I locked my bedroom door, set the lamp on the dresser and went to the window. The panes were rattling from the force of the wind and I could make out the bleak skeletons of the dead trees, as the wind whipped their naked branches, making them shriek as if in pain. I undressed and placed a quilted robe, plus sheepskin-lined slippers at my bedside in case I had to get up to investigate any disturbance during the night.

I went to the dresser to bring the lamp to my bedside table, when I felt a definite movement of the castle. It seemed to shudder in protest at the violence of the storm which was battering it. Then the lamp began to slide off the dresser. I reached out and seized it with both hands. A medium-sized jar of cream started a course toward the edge of the dresser. Just before it reached it, it seemed to give a little jump and went over the side.

The floor seemed to slant and I had to steady myself; I was off balance. The control I'd kept over my nerves was fast disappearing, for the moaning I'd heard before once again filled the room. A rocker began to move back and forth, as if it contained a contented spinster, patiently knitting away. I thought of Sarah Dexter and wondered if she'd ever sat in that chair.

I set the lamp on the night table, slipped into my robe and pushed my feet into the hard-soled slippers. I picked up the lamp again and moved carefully to the door, for the floor was still on the slant and I feared a shift in the opposite direction would throw me off balance. When I unlocked the door and stepped into the corridor, I was really frightened—but I saw no one, nothing. There was only darkness of an intensity not easily banished by the meager light of my lamp.

Opposite my room, a door suddenly popped open. It was as if it had been seized from the other side and yanked open to terrify me. It did—I screamed.

The ancient house seemed to be alive. There were sounds everywhere and always that moaning and groaning that seemed to come from walls, floors and ceilings. It was impossible to determine its source.

My outraged nerves received a final jolt when I heard a loud creaking sound from down the corridor. I raised the lamp to see better, though hopeful I'd not confront anyone.

At the far end of the hall, I saw what seemed to be a yawning aperture in the paneled wall. It was the area next to the sewing room which had puzzled me, for I'd felt there must be a room there. Apparently there was, though at the time, I'd not been able to find any evidence of one. However, there was now a definite space. No one appeared, yet it seemed as if someone must have opened it. Was it a trap to excite my curiosity and lure me to that room? And what sort of room, I wondered.

I walked deliberately toward it, for I suddenly remembered Miss Mary and wondered if she might be playing a little joke on me. I cautioned myself it could also be someone bent on murdering me. Yet I couldn't return to the sanctuary of my room without investigating it. The scientist in me had taken over. What puzzled me must be explored and studied. I even felt a trace of satisfaction that I'd been right in believing there had to be something behind that wall. Now I knew there was. A secret room!

But when I reached it, there was nothing but paneled wall. Annoyed, I used my free hand to pound on the area where I estimated the opening had been. Nothing happened except that the door that had flown wide when

183

I opened my bedroom door, now slammed shut. Once again, the castle seemed to shudder and the moans and groans reverberated throughout it. Try as I might, I could no longer control my terror. I returned to my room, my knees threatening to collapse. I turned the lock, set the lamp on my bedside table and sat on the side of the bed.

I was ashamed of myself and my fear. I wanted mightily to run to Rog, but I knew better. He'd keep me at his cottage until morning when he'd return me to the village. From there, he'd see to it I was headed homeward. I didn't want that.

I looked at the wall in my bedroom which opened to lead to the attic stairway. I picked up my lamp, went over to the candelabrum, pulled it forward and watched the paneled section open sufficiently to allow me to slip through. I walked slowly to it, stepped into the narrow hallway which led either to the pantry or to the attic. Slowly, I mounted the attic stairs, frightened but determined. The rain pounded the roof with a deafening din. I walked the length of the attic, searching for any sign of someone who might have hidden here. There was nothing. I studied the trunks. They were locked. Nothing was disturbed. The moans certainly didn't emanate from this room.

I returned to my room, pushed the candelabrum back into place and watched the panel close. I carried the lamp to the window. It threw illumination out onto one of the dead trees. While I watched, a large branch snapped off and slammed against the house, just missing the window before which I stood. It was almost as if Sarah Dexter was abroad, venting her anger on the island.

I'd listened to such a cacophony of noise that I was no longer affected by it. The fear I'd felt was replaced by exhaustion. I blew out my lamp and got back into bed. The sheets were icy cold, but it didn't seem to matter. Nothing mattered as I drifted off into sleep.

Rog came over to the castle early and while we breakfasted, I told him about the sounds I'd heard and my unsuccessful search for their source. I also mentioned the paneled wall in the upstairs corridor and how I'd believed I'd seen an opening there, but when I went to investigate, there was nothing. He attributed it to the play of light and shadow caused by the lamplight. But when I insisted, he accompanied me upstairs and I pointed out the area, emphasizing the fact there was no room behind the wall and so the space was unaccounted for.

He spent an hour trying to find an opening of some kind which would lead into it. He finally agreed the only way we'd learn what was behind it was to chop a hole in the paneling which, of course, was impossible without first getting permission from Mr. Upton. That too, wouldn't be likely, since he didn't want me here in the first place.

Rog left for his cottage then, telling me to be ready in about an hour. He was red-eyed from lack of sleep, mute evidence he'd kept a watch on the castle all night, something I'd not wanted him to do. I appreciated his concern, yet how could he expect we'd learn what this was all about, if I didn't make myself vulnerable? At any rate, he'd get an hour's sleep. I told him to make it two— that I'd not be ready before then. He nodded, quite agreeable.

I'd just completed making my bed and dusting my room, when I heard a car approaching the castle. I glanced out my window and saw the front seat contained two men. I couldn't make out who they were.

I was downstairs just as a firm knock sounded on the door. I opened it to confront Mr. Abrams and Mr. Tabor. I'd been here long enough to know that either of them could mean trouble, though I pretended not to notice the grimness of their features.

I said, "Good morning, gentlemen. Please come in."

"No time for it, Miss Dexter," Mr. Abrams said. "Just

came to warn you, the village folks are really mad at you."

"Now what have I done?" I asked.

"Really nothing, Miss Dexter," Mr. Tabor said. "But they're of a mind that you've done plenty."

Mr. Abrams said, "I went to the inn to warn you about the meeting they were holding and to drive you out here so you could get your boat and go to the mainland, but Mr. Tabor said you didn't return there. He figured you'd come back here."

"I did, gentlemen," I said. "My apparatus is here and I forgot about the time until the storm broke. I certainly couldn't return then."

Mr. Abrams said, "You promised Mr. Upton you wouldn't live here. I'm real scared the castle is going to be burned down. Mr. Upton ain't gonna like it one bit— 'specially since you told him you'd clear out."

Mr. Tabor said, "You'd really better, Miss Dexter. The men are holdin' a meetin' this very minute and they're real steamed up about you. Mr. Abrams don't want no more trouble on this island and neither do the owners of the inn. They called me last night to get firsthand information on what was going on."

"Nothing's going on, Mr. Tabor. You know my reason for being here."

He nodded. "Wish you could convince the villagers, but it's too late now. They're in an ugly mood."

"I'm beginning to get a little angry myself," I said. "Particularly since I've done nothing to antagonize them."

"Afraid you have, Miss Dexter," Mr. Abrams said. "Word's gone around that you're going to get the water condemned around here. They're at the town hall now having a talk about what to do. There are some who want to come here and burn you out."

"That's a vicious rumor and it's untrue. Who started it?"

"I don't know," he replied.

"Do you, Mr. Tabor?" I asked.

"I didn't even know 'bout the meetin' 'til Josh here came to the inn and told me 'bout it. I said I'd drive out with him and see if I couldn't convince you to take your boat and clear out. My wife'll pack your clothes—those few you brought back to the inn—and we'll ship them to wherever you say."

So they'd checked my room. I said, "I'm going to the village and talk with these people. They must listen to me."

"I wouldn't advise it," Mr. Abrams said.

"I didn't ask for your advice," I said. "Will you give me a ride back, please?"

"Certainly, Miss Dexter," he said. "I only hope you're not asking for more trouble. You got enough as it is."

Inwardly I agreed. "I'll get my jacket and be right with you."

In a minute I was in the back seat and the car was headed for the village. I glanced at Rog's cottage and wished mightily he knew about the latest trouble, but it was as well he didn't. He too might be against my confrontation with the villagers, but I'd had enough of bigotry and antagonism and, yes—ignorance. It seemed to me as if the ride was endless, but when I urged Mr. Tabor to greater speed, he replied he wasn't inclined to break a spring and it would be an easy thing to do. So I sat back and concentrated on what I could say to convince these people my work would do them only good.

We finally stopped in front of the small town hall. A white frame structure with double doors and a steeple, it resembled a church more than a civic auditorium. A few children were clustered on the steps; small groups of women gathered on the sidewalk. The children stopped their chattering and ogled me curiously. I wondered if they'd been told I was the descendant of Sarah Dexter, witch, because as I approached the steps, they scattered,

187

making a clear path. The glances of the women were openly hostile.

Neither Mr. Abrams nor Mr. Tabor accompanied me inside, stating they had to get back to their work. I didn't mind. I doubted very much I had an ally in either, and I had to win or lose on my own. I opened the door and entered. Though there was room for at least two hundred people in here, there were no more than twenty-five men present. I walked briskly down the aisle, my head high. Only by revealing confidence would I get a hearing. There was one man on the stage who had obviously been haranguing the others, because there was open antagonism in the eyes of the listeners as they turned to regard me.

"We got company, men," the speaker on the dais said. "None other than the descendant of the witch Sarah Dexter. Suppose you've come here to put a curse on us. As if you ain't done so already."

I went up the steps and walked across the stage to the speaker. "You know who I am, but I don't know your name."

"Hal Prentice," he said. "You're a fool for coming here."

"I'd be a bigger fool if I didn't," I replied calmly. "I'm sick and tired of being persecuted."

"You persecuted?" he asked. "What do you say to that, men?"

A man seated in the first row, stood up. "You're doin' the persecutin', ma'am. Deprivin' us of a livin'."

"That isn't true," I replied.

"Didn't you say these waters are so polluted, it's not safe to eat the fish?" he asked.

"I did," I replied. "Tests I've made of the channel waters show them heavily poisoned with mercury. Part of it's been coming from the plant owned by the Mayne family. However, I've been assured they're already taking

188

steps to stop the dumping of these poisons into the channel."

"But you're still sayin' we shouldn't fish there."

"If I didn't say it now, someone else would eventually, and then you might not be able to fish there for some time—if ever."

He thought about that a moment. "What about deep water?"

"The deeper, the better. I haven't found that the pollution exists in deep water here—at least, that composed of mercury compounds."

Mr. Prentice said, "You going to bring the government down on us if we fish the channel?"

I smiled. "I'm afraid none of you know why I'm really here."

"Yes, we do, Miss Dexter," another man called out from the audience. "We think you're here to get even."

"What do you mean?"

He stood up and I noticed he was older than the others. I doubted he could be a commercial fisherman. "Just this. You been here long enough to have heard the story of Sarah Dexter and what the islanders tried to do to her."

"I've heard the story—several versions of it, in fact."

"Nonetheless, it happened."

"You mean that the islanders went to the castle with the intent purpose of lynching her."

"That's right," came the placid reply. "Only they couldn't find her. No one ever saw hide nor hair of her again."

"What does that have to do with me?"

"You're one of her descendants and you've come back to get even with us."

If the situation hadn't been so serious, I'd have laughed.

"I doubt very much I'm a descendant of Sarah Dexter. But even if I should be, I'm not here to hurt any of you.

My idea is to help you. Besides, my work here has been connected with my education. I wish to acquire a higher degree in marine biology. What I've discovered here, I'll write into a thesis."

"Then you're not fillng a report to prevent us from fishing?"

"Certainly not. But I want to say this, if you and your families continue to eat fish from these waters over a period of time, you'll bring upon yourself the possibility of a long and dangerous illness. Mercury enters the liver and builds up there. When enough is present, you become very ill. I assure you, gentlemen, I am not exaggerating the seriousness of the situation."

No one made an immediate answer, and I could see from their faces that they were giving serious thought to what I'd said. I looked at Hal Prentice. He too looked pensive.

"Well, gentlemen?" I asked.

Mr. Prentice said, "What you say, Miss Dexter, makes sense. It's been in the papers and on television. Only we didn't think it was in these parts. So we'll wait."

"To burn down the witch's house or start fishin' again?" Another of the men called from the audience.

"Simmer down, Buck," Mr. Prentice said. "I say we ask government experts to come in and make tests and we'll go along with their findings."

My smile was one of relief. "Thank you, Mr. Prentice."

"I ain't finished yet, Miss Dexter," he said. "Maybe we're wrong—but we don't want you on the island."

"You can say that again," the same voice called. He was a big, rough-looking man, and he was regarding me with contempt. "We don't want witches on the island. You're as big a troublemaker as Sarah Dexter was."

I said, "My work here is completed and I intend to leave shortly."

"The quicker, the better, Miss Dexter." Mr. Prentice spoke quietly, but I knew he meant what he said.

I nodded, turned and walked across the stage to the stairs. As I started down the aisle, the burly man arose and pointed a finger at me.

"You be out of Witch's Castle by sundown or we'll be out there to burn it down. Maybe it wouldn't burn before, but it will now. Times have changed."

I paused, looked him directly in the eyes and said quietly, "Sometimes I wonder, sir."

I went outside, not even glancing at the women still assembled on the sidewalk. I had no idea how I'd get back to the castle. I'd certainly not ask either Mr. Abrams or Mr. Tabor to drive me back. There was no taxi service out of season. There was nothing to do but walk. I consulted the tide chart pasted to the window of Mr. Abram's tackle shop. With luck, I'd make it before the tide started in.

I felt hollow inside. Tonight, Witch's Castle would be burned down. A few men could do it. I felt certain that this time, it would not withstand the torches put to it. I wondered what twist of fate had caused me to choose Witch's Island as a place to earn my thesis. And by twist of fate, I didn't mean Sarah Dexter. I could now better understand Miss Mary's compassion for the poor woman who had endured such persecution. Miss Mary had earned only scorn and a cruel nickname; I had earned hatred.

TWENTY-ONE

I was nearing the outskirts of the village when I heard the sound of a loud motor. Roger was riding his motorbike toward me at top speed. He saw me, slowed down and came to a stop alongside me.

"What are you doing at the village—and how'd you get there?"

"Mr. Abrams and Mr. Tabor came to the castle to warn me to take my boat and go to the mainland. The natives are restless."

"What's it all about?"

"Briefly, they thought I was going to issue a report to prevent them from fishing in these waters."

"Did you straighten them out on that?"

"Yes, but they still want me off the island. They believe I'm a descendant of Sarah Dexter and they're threatening to burn the castle down."

He looked grim. "Hop on. I'll take you back."

I obeyed. "Before you start, Rog, just one thing. I'm ready to leave, but I'll not be driven out. I've done nothing wrong. Besides, I'm more concerned than ever about Miss Mary."

"So am I," he admitted. "I wish she'd go back to Boston."

I slipped my arms around his waist and rested my head against his shoulder. "She's as stubborn as I."

"And almost as lovable. Hang on. Here we go."

I'd never ridden a two-wheeler before, and though it was bumpy, it was also fun. I was almost sorry when we reached the castle, until Rog said he was going to do some deep diving.

"Please let me come," I said. "It's safer with two and it will take my mind off the unpleasantness I've just been through."

"Get into your suit," he said. "I'll meet you at the pier."

"What will you investigate this time?"

"The water just off the island nearest the castle."

"Why?"

"Something must undermine the end of the island to make this house tremble and shudder as it does—at least, as you described it."

"It's true."

"And it would have to be caused by a movement of the earth," he went on. "No force of wind or rain, tide or waves, could do that unless . . ." his voice trailed off momentarily, then took on excitement, as a sudden idea came to him. ". . . unless the water gets under the house during a storm."

"But how could it?" I asked. "I don't see how it's possible for the sea to reach beneath the castle unless it's there all the time. If there is a channel under the

194

tip of the island, it must be constantly filled with water and the house would tremble constantly."

"You'll grant that water rushing in and out of a cavern could make the house shake."

"Yes. And make doors fly open and slam shut and tilt the house enough so that objects would slide . . . Rog, that must be it."

He nodded. "The water in that area is so shallow, I never bothered to go into it. No yacht could get within half a mile of that side of the island."

"What yacht?"

"The one I'm looking for," he said. "Now stop asking questions and get your gear."

I reached the pier first and was attaching my flippers when he returned, carrying face mask, flippers, tank and, this time, an underwater lamp which I hadn't even known he possessed. I made no comment and we hastily attached the flippers, waddled to the edge of the pier, pulled on our face masks and hoisted the air tanks into a more comfortable position. He caught my hand and squeezed it lightly just before he stepped off the pier and plunged into the water.

I followed him at once. We struck out in a direction opposite our former explorations. It was quite shallow here. The bottom presented me with several interesting forms of aquatic life, but I didn't stop to harvest any. Rog was moving on at a steady rate, swimming close to the bottom.

The water began to grow murky. There was mud on the bottom and the sea was keeping it stirred up as waves splashed against solid substance, instead of quietly rolling in.

Through the brownish-colored water, I saw what looked like the side of a craggy mountainside. Not mountainous itself, for it rose not more than twenty feet, not quite enough to clear the surface of the water even at low tide.

Rog swam back and pointed in the direction from which he'd come. I was to follow. He switched on his underwater lamp and that helped me keep track of him. I swam in his wake until both he and the light vanished mysteriously.

My momentary fear was ended when the light reached me again, turned straight in my face. I swam on and discovered that he had found a large hole in the side of the underwater cliff. It was the opening of a cave. I swam on through and, once clear of the opening, we went down toward the bottom again. We kept swimming for a considerable distance until we found ourselves in a rock-lined pool.

He dove to the bottom and played his light about inquiringly. I swam to his side and we both searched. I didn't know for what, but he was so intent on the task, I felt I could do no less.

We were on our way back when he discovered the four steel drums near the opening into this pool. They were imbedded in the mud so that not more than a foot of their tops could be seen. Apparently they'd been guided to the opening of the cave somehow, then pushed through and allowed to fall to the floor of the cave. The existence of the cave was unknown, so this made the perfect hiding place.

He tapped my arm and waved the lamp toward the cave opening. He preceded me and we swam on through. Presently, we bobbed up beside the pier. He hauled himself out of the water, grasped my hand and pulled me up. We shed our flippers and face masks and removed our tanks. He looked pleased.

"Did you find what you were looking for?" I asked.

"Exactly what I've spent weeks trying to find. And we've solved two mysteries with the same dive. Two puzzles just fell into place."

"I'd like to know what they are," I said. "Though I

think I know what you mean when you connect that underwater cave with the manifestations at the house."

"We know that people always fled from the castle after a storm. You too found that the moaning and creaking, the movements of inanimate objects, doors opening and slamming shut, happened then. The tides were high, the waves strong. They pounded through that cave opening and slammed into the rock walls of the cave. The castle is built directly above. The power behind crashing waves is tremendous. It's enough to have caused the cave walls to shake, and so the castle shook, right to its foundations. The moaning and groaning came from pockets of air trapped under the castle. As it rushed in and out, compressed by the waves, it made roaring sounds that were reduced to moans and groans by the cave walls and the foundation of the house."

"There's a dry well in the basement," I recalled. "It must go almost down to the roof of the cave and it could capture those sounds perfectly and broadcast them as if through a horn." I smiled. "I feel foolish when I think of how it terrified me."

He grinned. "I guess we've put an end to the spooky manifestations."

I was peering out to sea. "There's a large boat of some kind heading our way."

"Let's go."

He dropped our tanks into the motorboat, caught my hand and we fled to his cottage. There, he took a rifle out of a closet and went to a window. I stood beside him while we tried to identify the oncoming craft.

"It's Libby Mayne's launch," I exclaimed.

"You're right."

"Do you think it's odd that she happened to be nearby when we came out of the water?"

"She wasn't that near. She seems to be alone. We'll wait a few more minutes before we go out to meet her."

197

As she brought the craft in, we went out to the pier. She eased alongside and threw Rog a rope. He caught it, wound it around a piling and she jumped ashore.

She looked stunning in white slacks and sweater, with a yachtsman's cap over her hair. But concern etched her features as she spoke.

"I telephoned the inn, Gale, and Mr. Tabor told me you were back at the castle, but you were leaving the island. Thank goodness I caught you. I've discovered something horrible."

"What?" I asked.

"Ten miles above our outflow pipe," she said, "about ten thousand fish are floating on the surface, all dead. Whatever killed them couldn't have come from our pipe. The tide carries the waste in an opposite direction, but I have a feeling we're going to be blamed for those dead fish. The water must be polluted with something mighty lethal. I think you should investigate it."

"So do I," I said.

Rog said, "I'll go along."

"Stay in your diving clothes," I said. "I'll need a few minutes to get supplies from my lab. Oh—were the fish dead when first seen?"

"Yes. They were discovered on the surface at dawn. I suppose they were killed during the night. Must have been a school of them and a big one. You can hardly see the water for the layer of dead fish."

"Did you see them yourself?"

"Yes . . . I went up there immediately, once word was brought to me. When I couldn't reach you in the village, I came here."

"Were the fish bloated?"

"Yes. They reminded me of blowfish, but they're not."

"You can lead the way," I said. "Rog and I will follow in my boat. I won't be but a few minutes."

I did take time to get out of my diving suit and into

198

a slacks outfit. Downstairs, I got what I needed to take samples of water, then I returned to the boat.

Rog had the motor running and we roared in the wake of Libby's larger and faster craft. I was trying to determine, in my mind, where the poison had come from. A large quantity of it must have been dumped at one time; otherwise, the sea would have diluted it sufficiently that all those fish wouldn't have been killed at the same time. Where it might have originated, was beyond my comprehension. We were now ten miles above the channel —certainly too far from Libby's chemical factory for it to have disposed of the poison which had killed the fish, and there was no river water coming into the ocean at that point.

"I don't understand it," I said to Roger, shouting above the roar of the engine and the wind.

"What don't you understand?" he shouted back.

"How any kind of poison got to a point ten miles up the coast. Unless there's some factory there I don't know of. Yet, if there is and they dumped waste into the sea before, I'd have known it from the samples I took down the coast."

"Why not wait until we get there. Perhaps then we can determine exactly what did happen."

He was right. "Are you some kind of policeman?"

"Why?"

"You think like one."

"I told you, I'm in the insurance business."

"You're not going to try to make me believe you insured a shipment of illicit drugs."

He smiled. "Well, no. I don't think our actuaries would stand for it. I'll fill you in on all the details later. Too hard to talk here."

I had to agree. It took a full hour to reach the spot where Libby's boat began to slow down and she signaled for us to come alongside. As we did, she pointed toward the coast and there I saw the dead fish. The sea was covered with them. At several places, the water was boiling as big predators came in for the banquet—which would kill them before long. I knew that scavenger crabs would be feasting on the dead fish and they too would die. So would every other form of sea life, and there'd be a great many, for these dead fish would be consumed in some way or another in a matter of a few days. Death was sweeping a wide path through this part of the ocean.

At my direction, Rog sent the boat moving slowly through the mass of dead fish. Libby was right; they were bloated. I took several of them out of the water and provided myself with samples of the water as well.

"I'll signal Libby to follow us," I said. "I want to go to her factory."

"What for?"

"She has a complete laboratory and chemists there who can tell me what killed the fish in short order."

"Whatever you wish," he said.

He backed out of the area of dead fish. In clearer water, he turned the prow of the boat toward land, some two or three miles below us. I waved to Libby and motioned back in the direction from which we'd come. She nodded, turned and moved ahead of us.

TWENTY-TWO

Libby awaited us at her dock. She gave me a hand up while Rog secured the boat.

"What do you think happened?" she asked.

"I don't know yet. Will your laboratory analyze the water and the organs of the fish?"

"Immediately," she said. "All I hope is that we don't get blamed for that kill."

"It isn't possible that waste from your factory could have spread up that far. Even if it had, it would have been extremely diluted by the time it got there and would have taken days, perhaps weeks, before fish died from the poison. This hit them like a bolt of lightning."

Rog said he'd remain with the boat, so Libby led me to a white-painted building, part of the factory, but separate from it. Here I found a modern, well-equipped laboratory and enough highly skilled chemists to do the analytical work quickly.

"I don't think DDT did it," I explained to the chief chemist. "It worked too fast, but you might check for chlordane and toxaphene."

He removed the stopper from the bottle of sea water and sniffed. "Did you smell of this?"

"No, I merely collected it. There was no odor of chemicals at sea." I smelled of the contents and I looked up sharply. "How about benzene hexachloride?"

He nodded. "I think you hit it. This won't take long. Half an hour."

"I'll be back then," I said. I turned to Libby. "Nobody's going to blame you for this, so stop worrying."

"I'd better tell my dad. Will you excuse me?"

"Of course. I'll be out with Rog."

I boarded the motorboat and sat down beside him. "We think we detected the nature of the chemical by the odor coming from the sea water I sampled. It's a potent chemical that comes in powder form and it's murder on marine life."

"How much time do we have?" he asked.

"About half an hour."

"Time enough to fill you in on a few details. I do work for an insurance company. My dad is one of the executives there. We had insured a yacht for a million and a half. We do a great deal of maritime insurance and this didn't seem like any unusual deal. But we keep track of those heavily insured boats and, in this case, we discovered the yacht was making too many trips between too many ports where drugs could easily be had."

"Who owns it?" I asked.

"A corporation. They often use covers for illicit work. The registry is in the name of an import-export firm. We've

202

tried to track down the officers, but it's impossible. The boat is registered abroad and you either can't get the records there, or there aren't any. We did hear the yacht was being used in smuggling drugs, mostly heroin, because that's where the biggest profit is. If this is true, then the insurance is void."

"Where is the yacht now?"

"It sank some months ago. According to the last radio message received from it, they were about five hundred miles off Boston, but I think they radioed a false location. Possibly because they thought they might be able to make port without assistance. We think she was just off the point of Witch's Island when the call was sent out. Informants told us she was supposed to be carrying a shipment of heroin, the pure stuff. So I volunteered to try and find the ship."

"But if they gave their position as five hundred miles away, why do you think they were much closer to shore?" I asked.

"A freighter saw the yacht. It was just plain luck that they got word to us that the yacht was moving slowly away from the point, but did not seem to be in any trouble. I hope she sank within a diver's range."

I was still puzzled. "But the containers in the cave under the castle. Could that have been the yacht's cargo?"

"We think so. Interpol, an international police agency, informed us that they believed rival drug smugglers had hidden aboard to take over the yacht. Maybe that happened; we're not sure. The only thing I'm fairly certain of is that the yacht reached the point and divers disposed of the cargo by placing it in the underwater cave which, I think, they did regularly. It would be safe there no matter how great the storm, and amateur divers, even professionals, hired to look for the stuff, would never find it.

Your experience at the castle provided the tip I needed. Then, after the cargo was safe, the yacht put out to sea again because they didn't want this disposal point known to anyone. It must have been afterward that it sunk. How, I don't know."

"Well," I said, "you've apparently found the dope. Now you've got to find the yacht."

"The policy—like most—states plainly that, if the craft is used for any kind of illicit work, the policy is void. We don't like paying out a million and a half if we don't have to, especially to a ring of drug peddlers."

"Now I understand why you were so secretive about your work and stayed to yourself."

He smiled. "I kind of like breathing. Besides, if this turned into something tough, I didn't want you involved. The price was too high. Those four steel vats were mostly filled with cement to keep them on the bottom, and stable, but there was enough room left to hide two hundred and ten pounds of pure heroin. Now, before you think that's a small haul, let me say that the retail value of that much heroin, properly cut, is worth three million dollars."

"I believe it."

"As I told you, informers provided most of the information about the shipment, so we know its size and importance. Three million is a lot of money, even to drug smugglers. It was safer not to give you an inkling of what I was doing here."

"And Sam Vernon, or whatever his real name was?"

"He's why we think there may have been stowaways who were after the shipment. Vernon was a member of a gang sworn to avenge a hijacking on the part of those who we think operated the yacht."

"And who might they be?" I asked.

"I don't know yet. However, someone on this island

must have received the goods and handled the cutting, which I'm sure was done in Witch's Castle. The only islander I suspect is involved, is Tabor. Although I've wondered about Mr. Abrams, who handled the rental of the place. He doesn't seem the type, but in this illicit business there are no types. Women too, are engaged in it, especially the smuggling angle."

"You still suspect her."

"Her friendliness could well be a method of trying to find out what you know. Her father has the best means to properly cut the stuff and then merchandise it to dealers all over the country. No one would suspect drug shipments from a legitimate chemical manufacturing business. Heroin looks like any other white powder and could be labeled as something else."

"I hope you're wrong. I like her."

"Her father is wealthy. Maybe this medium-sized plant makes a great deal of money. Or perhaps he acquired his wealth through other legitimate channels."

"How about Mr. Upton?" I asked.

"He certainly purchased the castle unexpectedly, and bid a price higher than the owner was asking. Upton is a legit businessman with a good reputation, but the higher-ups in this racket try to be upstanding citizens, so they'll never be suspected. I'm not writing him off."

I glanced at my watch. "I'd better get back to the lab. I won't be long if the tests came out properly."

They had a tentative report ready for me. It was benzene hexachloride, a chemical they were sure had not been used in Libby's plant, nor in any other manufacturing business along the coast. As I read the report, I began to understand the reason for the sacrifice of all those fish.

"Thank you," I told the chief chemist. "Tell Miss Mayne I'll contact her later."

Rog started the engine as I came aboard. I said, "It was a drug not used around here, which means it was deliberately dumped into the ocean. I wonder why."

"Probably to lure us away from the castle so a diver could get the narcotic. They must suspect our company is on to them."

"Do you suppose they suspect you?" I asked worriedly.

"I'm inclined to think they're more suspicious of you."

"You mean they believe I'm not really what I say I am?"

"I'm afraid that's it."

"I think I convinced the villagers I was telling the truth."

"That may be what has them worried. They can't depend on the villagers any more to scare you away. They have to act now—and fast."

"What are you going to do?"

"I'm going to see if the containers are still in the cave beneath the castle. If they are, I'm sending word to the proper authorities. They'll be here to retrieve them."

"You can't go down there alone."

"I can and I will. You're taking the boat to the mainland."

"I'll not leave without you," I said.

"What will you do?"

"Return to the castle and bring my luggage and equipment back to the boat. After you surface, you can dress and we'll go to the village or the mainland."

"It better be the mainland."

"What about Miss Mary?"

"What about her?"

"We can't leave her here."

"I don't believe they'll bother her. They know she has no suspicion that there's anything wrong going on here."

"I wouldn't be so sure. She might know a great deal more than we suspect. Even you admit she's clever."

"Clever enough to outwit them, I'll bet."

"I hope so," I said fervently.

I estimated we'd been gone three hours. It would take another hour to get back. Four hours had been lost. We might be too late. Neither Roger nor I spoke until we were within sight of the pier and the stark, dreary-looking castle which dominated the point. He still wore his diving suit and I took a turn at the wheel so he could get into the rest of his diving gear.

The moment I brought the boat to the pier, he kissed me briefly, put on his face mask, checked to see his equipment was in working order, then jumped into the water.

I walked to the castle, worried about him, praying he'd encounter no one in the cave. The dwelling looked bleak and dismal. I dreaded entering it and wished the door would open and I'd see a smiling Miss Mary waiting to greet me. The sight of her cheery features would do much to reassure me and help me over the waiting period until Rog returned.

I went into the kitchen and packed the rest of my laboratory equipment, then I went upstairs to pack my clothes and diving suit. I snapped my bags shut and placed them outside the door. I reentered the room for a final look around to make certain I'd not forgotten anything. Passing a window, I caught a glimpse of two men. I moved back quickly so I'd not be in view, but they were still in my line of vision. It was Mr. Upton and Mr. Tabor. The former seemed to be issuing orders, for the latter nodded from time to time. Then Mr. Tabor started around the house. Mr. Upton took a key from his pocket and moved in a direct path to the front entrance.

I heard a door close softly and a few fast-moving footsteps in the corridor. Someone was on this floor. My door was open, but no one appeared. I knew Mr. Tabor was going to come in the back entrance and Mr. Upton the front. I had to find someplace to conceal myself. I didn't doubt but that they'd seen me enter and I felt certain their mission was to see I didn't leave.

I stepped into the hall and looked around. There wasn't a sign of anyone. Then I heard the front door close softly, followed by whispered voices. Both men were now inside and were going to institute a search for me. I looked about, desperate for a place to hide. I thought of the secret passage leading to the attic, but certainly they'd search there.

My heart pounded madly and I felt like a trapped animal, with the hunters closing in for the kill. I could think of nothing else to do but confront them, bluff my way out of this predicament. They didn't know what I knew. Not unless they'd learned who Rog really was and why he was here. I heard a pair of footsteps start to ascend the stairs. They moved cautiously, as if they believed I still had no awareness of their presence. I stood there, my eyes darting about, still seeking some avenue of escape.

I thought I heard a soft hissing sound and I looked to my left. A narrow aperture was opened. It was the paneled area which revealed no room behind it and which Rog and I had inspected so carefully without success. I moved swiftly toward it, stepped in. It closed immediately and soundlessly. Not a sliver of light dispelled the blackness and, by the same token, no air seemed to penetrate it either, for the place had a rank, dead, musty odor.

I didn't move, fearful Tabor and Upton would hear me. I felt reasonably safe—unless it was they or one of their cohorts who'd opened this aperture, thus setting a trap into which I'd walked.

I could hear their muted talking. Apparently, they'd thrown caution to the winds and were now either irritated or worried they'd not captured me. I resigned myself to stand there in the blackness, grateful for the sanctuary I'd found. I only hoped Rog was in no danger, either below or once he'd surfaced, hoping it was I whom Upton and Tabor were after. Yet Rog *was* in danger, particularly if they'd learned his identity. And certainly, if they'd observed him diving, he must have aroused their suspicion.

TWENTY-THREE

Apparently they were on the other side of the wall, for I could make out what they were saying, though their voices sounded far away, mute testimony that the walls were thick.

Tabor said, "I stood in this hall every minute you were inspecting the rooms. She couldn't have got away."

"She's a highly trained scientist and clever as hell," Upton said.

"Too damned clever. I'd like to wring her neck."

"Let's get her first. I want to use her to compel Randall to sit tight until we reclaim that shipment. He's been diving so much, he must have found it."

"What is he anyway?" Tabor asked.

"I don't know. If he was a narco agent, he'd have a small army here by now. If he was regular police, the same thing would have happened. I figure he's some kind of private investigator."

"Maybe he was working with Vernon," Tabor suggested.

"Never mind the talk. I'm going to check the attic. Don't move from this spot."

"Door leading to it's downstairs."

"I know where it is," came the caustic reply.

Apparently they didn't know about the secret entrance to the stairway from my bedroom. I moved away from the wall, feeling reasonably secure, wishing only for a breath of fresh air. But I tensed with renewed alarm, for I had no idea how the panel had opened. Could I have stepped on a certain board and caused it to do so? I knew it had opened the night of the storm also. Was it the shifting of the castle that had caused it? Would it be possible Tabor or Upton might step on a board or lean against something that would slide the panel back? I had to know where I was in case just such a thing occurred. It might be there was another exit from this room. Upton's voice calling Tabor, made me stop in my tracks.

"Where the hell do you suppose Randall is?"

"We know he went up the coast with the Dexter dame to check on the dead fish. He musta come back with her."

"We know he's not in his cottage and he sure didn't take that motorbike back to the village. Nobody'll ride that again."

Tabor said, "Maybe you better get your diving gear from my car and go down. Take your spear gun down too. Better not miss this time."

"I won't. First though, I'd like to find that dame. Let's check downstairs again. Might be a closet or a cabinet of some kind we missed. We've also got to immobilize that boat."

I could hear them moving rapidly down the corridor. At least they were no longer a few inches from where I stood. I took a step forward with my hands outstretched for the initial encounter with the dim objects I could barely make out. I discovered a wooden chair and ran my hands up and down the back of it to make sure I'd identified it properly. My thigh brushed against the edge of what seemed to be a table. My hand moved along the edge, then continued to explore its surface. I touched what seemed to be a large book. I was like a blind person, depending upon my fingertips to identify each object as I touched it.

It seemed to be a fairly large table and I made my way partly around it, still testing the surface for more objects. I found a stub of a candle in a holder. Then my fingers encountered something I could not identify. A fairly long, narrow, round object about the circumference of a broom handle, I thought.

I let go of the object and reached in my slacks outfit for a pack of matches. I lit one and applied it to the wick. A tiny flame came to life, sputtered a few times and finally the aged wax began to burn properly. I picked up the candlestick holder and as I turned around, I held it high.

I stood rooted to the spot, unable to scream or cry out, though terror flowed in waves through me. The room was barren of furniture except for a chair and a table. But still seated in the chair and arrayed over part of the table, was a human skeleton. I'd actually touched an arm bone when my hand investigated the table in the darkness. But that wasn't all I saw.

Standing behind the skeleton was Miss Mary, a benign smile on her face. She was mad—stark, raving mad. She'd lured me in here moments ago. I wished suddenly I'd confronted Tabor and Upton in the castle proper. I might have outwitted them. Now I was trapped.

"Don't be frightened," she said softly. "Sarah Dexter can't hurt you."

My eyes flicked to the skeleton, still partially draped with clothes.

"Yes, that's Miss Sarah Dexter," Miss Mary went on. "I'll not let anyone harm her."

I thought of the nickname the villagers had given this gentle lady whom both Rog and I had regarded so highly. Her gentleness had fooled us, but not the villagers.

I breathed deeply to regain a degree of calmness and started to back away, but the room was small and I'd taken only a few steps when my spine made contact with the wall.

Miss Mary regarded me sadly. "You think I'm insane, don't you? Shame on you, dear. I've sheltered you. This is a sanctuary. It was Sarah Dexter's sanctuary."

"She died in here." I found my voice.

Miss Mary nodded and motioned to the open Bible. "Read what she wrote in the Bible." When I didn't move, she said, "Come, Gale. I won't hurt you. Even if I'm mad, I'm gentle. Come over here and read Sarah Dexter's last words."

Though stiff-legged, I went over. Dust covered the open pages of the Bible. I held the candle close to the book, bent over and read the few lines written in a fine hand.

I pray they be forgiven if I die at their hands or in this room which I fear will become my tomb. Of witchcraft I know naught. All I do know is in this Bible which I have read many times outside this room and scant times within it, for I must husband the only candle I have. I have been gravely ill and I fear that my time has come. Would that they had waited a day longer so that I might have died in my bed and been accorded a decent burial. Pray for me.

Sarah Dexter

So this was Sarah Dexter, reputed to be a witch and the intended subject of a lynching. Evidently she'd known the mob was on its way and, though desperately ill, had taken refuge in this secret room.

I closed my eyes and offered the prayer she had requested. Then, as if the shock of the discovery overcame me again, I screamed. Over and over and over. Miss Mary was trying to shush me and when she placed a hand on my arm, I brushed her off, dropping the candle and plunging the room once again into stygian darkness. But my hysterics had been heard by Upton and Tabor. I covered my mouth and held my breath. It was the only way I could stop.

I'd backed away and was leaning against the wall again, but Tabor and Upton were calling my name and pounding on the wall. The sounds were muted and though at first close, they seemed to move farther away. Apparently, they didn't know exactly where I was. They'd not hit upon the idea of a secret room.

Then a match was struck and I saw Miss Mary. She'd retrieved the candle and touched its flame to the wick.

"Don't be frightened," she said softly. "Contrary to what you believe, I am *not* mad. I found this secret room one day when I was cleaning the corridor walls. When I discovered poor Sarah Dexter here, I knew I couldn't allow the villagers to know. They already considered me odd because I felt compassion for the young people who came here. Some were very confused, I'll admit, but I let them talk and question me and I'd hope they'd listen when I answered their questions as best I could."

"What are you saying?" I asked.

"That I wanted the remains of this good woman to have a decent burial. I didn't want anyone to know about this room until I could be assured I could give her a proper burial."

The pounding on the wall was still angry and urgent,

but I paid it no mind. I went over to Miss Mary and took her in my arms.

"Forgive me," I said.

She smiled. "You're not frightened of me?"

"Not any more," I replied.

"When you saw me and I smiled, it was to reassure you. But I frightened you instead. I didn't mind those horrible men coming here because they kept people out of here. I feared one of the owners would eventually find this room. To me, this was a room to be revered. I can bury Sarah Dexter's remains now."

"If we get out of here alive," I said, motioning with my head toward the pounding and the angry shouting of the two men.

Miss Mary said, "It was Tabor who frightened you. He did the screaming and calling on Belial. He did it to others who either bought the castle or rented it. I knew evil men entered the castle from time to time, but I swear I didn't know what they did. I watched from my cottage mostly, though once they almost caught me in here and I had to take refuge in this room, just as Sarah Dexter did when the villagers came to lynch her."

Then the pounding stopped and I heard my name called. After that, came the terrifying sound of gunshots.

"Rog!" I cried out. "Let me out of here, Miss Mary. I must get out. He might be wounded or even—dead."

She went over to the wall, bent down and pulled open a section of board. As she did so, she said, "My dear Roger isn't dead, but Mr. Upton is. And Mr. Tabor has been shot in the leg."

The panel opened as she spoke and Rog again called my name. I stepped through the aperture into his arms. He was still holding his rifle, but Miss Mary took it from him and aimed it at Mr. Tabor who was on the floor, moaning and holding his knee.

216

Rog held me close for a minute and spoke my name over and over. Then he released me.

"Upton shot at me first. Tabor was also armed, but hadn't time to use his gun."

"How did you know they were here?"

"They were too sure of themselves. Tabor's car was parked at my cottage. They'd apparently checked to see if I was there. When I wasn't, they thought I'd be at the castle. They disabled the motorbike, then came here."

"They wanted to use me as a hostage to force you to let them get the narcotic. Then, I suppose, they'd have killed us both."

"Weighted us with cement and dropped us at sea," Rog said. He looked at the space through which Miss Mary and I had come. "So there is a secret room."

"Sarah Dexter's remains are there," I said and told him what the room contained. "Miss Mary discovered it some time ago."

"Five years ago," she said. She was still holding the gun on Tabor and didn't take her eyes from him while she spoke. Upton's lifeless form lay at the head of the stairs.

"I owe her my life," I said.

"We both owe our lives to her," Rog said. "If it hadn't been for that secret room, you'd have been captured and they'd have lain in wait for me."

I nodded. "They were going to disable the boat, but wanted to capture me first."

Rog said, "Miss Mary, how did you happen to be here?"

"I've been here quite a lot lately. I knew you were up to something and I was worried because I also knew Mr. Tabor and Mr. Upton and others who came here were also up to something. I was fearful they'd find Sarah Dexter's remains. I must see to her burial immediately."

217

I said, "May we attend the services with you, Miss Mary?"

"Yes, my dear, and I hope you'll allow me to attend your marriage."

Rog said, "You'll be seated with our families. Now I have to get to the village. I'll take Tabor with me. You and Miss Mary can go to her place. I'll use the boat. You can use his car."

TWENTY-FOUR

Sarah Dexter's remains were buried after a formal, religious funeral attended by everyone on the island. Her Bible, left open as it was found, was displayed under glass in the village's small museum for all to see and to read what she had written.

Tabor was held for trial on charges of smuggling and distributing drugs. Roger explained everything to Miss Mary and me when he rejoined us at her cottage after he'd delivered Tabor to the state police and given a report to them regarding the shooting at the castle.

"From what Tabor admitted—and he talked freely—my theories were mostly right. The yacht was sunk about eight miles due east of the point. Rival drug smugglers, one of whom was Sam Vernon, tried to hijack the cargo, but they were overpowered. The cargo was then dumped into the sea. Divers aboard the yacht transferred it to the cave as they always did. The yacht pulled away. By that time, the people who'd tried to take over, revealed there was a bomb aboard which would go off in a few minutes. There was no time to reach and defuse it. Everybody got into life boats . . . except those rival smugglers who were likely killed in a fight just before the bomb went off. A false radio signal was sent out, the yacht sank. The drug smugglers rowed ashore and were met by Tabor, who was their local agent. He put them up in the hotel as if they were visitors to the island."

"The hotel was certainly a handy place for those people," I said. Everything was becoming clear to me now.

"Upton, who headed the ring, decided that since Vernon and a couple of others got away, it might be best not to retrieve the shipment in the cave until Upton was positive the authorities hadn't been tipped off by the men who escaped. Then you arrived and moved into the castle. Tabor did his best to drive you away quickly. By burning your car; by entering the house and calling out to summon Satan; by that episode of a kettle of what was supposed to be a witch's brew. He shot at you when his other attempts failed. He hid in the sawgrass and kept track of everything through field glasses and a telescope. It was Upton, however, who took more drastic measures. He is an expert diver. It was he who tried to kill you with the spear gun. As for all the other manifestations, nature took care of them. The wind, the tides, and the sea linked up to shake the house itself and create all those ghostly sounds."

"I'm happy that Libby had nothing to do with it," I said.

"So am I. Though I can see they hoped we'd suspect her. When they suspected we'd found their cache of drugs, Upton arranged to have poison thrown into the sea so that we'd be drawn to the scene. Far enough away so they'd

220

have time to get the shipment out of the cave. As it happened, we came back too quickly."

"And Sam Vernon was trying to find the steel drums when he was killed," I said.

"Yes. He knew where they'd been dumped, but he didn't know about the cave. I'm sorry I had to keep my job here a secret, but there was a million and a half involved in the sinking of the yacht and three million in illicit drugs at stake. I was here for one purpose, to make sure the yacht had been carrying contraband and to find the drugs if possible. I had maps made, I checked the ocean bottom, I searched off the point until I despaired of ever finding what I looked for. My attaché case was filled with maps and estimates as to where the stuff might be. If Tabor or Upton had gotten their hands on it, I'd have been in Sam Vernon's fix. Then, with your help, I found the cave and the answer to the whole thing."

We left the island three days later. Though Rog and I had already said our farewells to Miss Mary, for we intended to return to the mainland by boat, on a sudden impulse we hiked to her cottage to ask if she would accompany us. To our surprise, she had just poured three glasses of sherry and opened the door with the bottle, still uncorked, in her hand.

"How did you know we were coming?" I asked.

"A melding of the minds, my dear," she replied in her serene way.

"Please come back with us," I said.

"Not for a few more days. I'm purchasing Witch's Castle and hope you'll rename it."

Rog said, "Why should we rename it?"

"Because it's to be my wedding present to you," she said. "And don't hurt me by refusing it."

She set the bottle on the tray and handed each of us a glass. Rog and I exchanged long glances. Then the three of us turned toward the fireplace. Without a word, we raised our glasses to the beautiful lady whose portrait hung above it. To Sarah Dexter, whose life had ended so tragically.

Why did we make the gesture? As Miss Mary would have put it—a melding of the minds.